Mary Elizabeth Maxwell

Under Love's Rule

Mary Elizabeth Maxwell

Under Love's Rule

ISBN/EAN: 9783337159115

Printed in Europe, USA, Canada, Australia, Japan

Cover: Foto ©Andreas Hilbeck / pixelio.de

More available books at **www.hansebooks.com**

BY THE AUTHOR OF

"LADY AUDLEY'S SECRET," "LONDON PRIDE," Etc.

LONDON

SIMPKIN, MARSHALL, HAMILTON, KENT & CO.
LIMITED

STATIONERS' HALL COURT

1897

———

[All rights reserved]

LONDON :

PRINTED BY WILLIAM CLOWES AND SONS, LIMITED,
STAMFORD STREET AND CHARING CROSS.

CONTENTS.

UNDER LOVE'S RULE.

CHAPTER I.

THE CHILDREN'S HOUR.

IT was teatime all over London; and it was the children's hour at No. 100, Palatine Square.

The children's hour. The words used to sound very pretty from the rosy lips of Mrs. Lerwick, the children's mother.

"Five o'clock is the children's hour," she would say. "They always have tea with me—when I am at home."

"The worst of it is that there are so few 'whens,'" Eustace, the eldest of the three boys, would complain sometimes.

For once in a way mother was at home. It was

B

early in the season, and the room seemed full of a
pale yellowness—the yellow of Lent lilies, the pale,
faint gold of an April sun.   It was mother's
morning room—on the second floor in Palatine
Square; and the flowers, the tables loaded with
silver toys, the Indian draperies, and tall painted
leather screen—on which Court beauties and Court
fops, after Watteau, danced a formal dance in a
formal garden—made up a prettier picture than the
spacious drawing-rooms below, with their six lofty
windows, and blue satin curtains, and immaculate
chintz chair-covers, and general air of being meant
for company.   Here the chair-covers were always
tumbled, the draperies were tossed about anyhow, and there were generally dogs on the
sofas.

Eustace, Paul, and Fritz loved the room; for it
was the only room in Palatine Square in which
they ever felt that their mother really belonged to
them and they to her.   In the country they saw
her nearly every day.   They ran behind her cart
when she drove her Norwegian ponies, dined now
and then at her luncheon-table, rode their shelties

to the meet with her when she made believe to follow the hounds; but in London mother was busy, with an air of incessant occupation which the Prime Minister himself could not have exceeded. This afternoon, even, though the tea-tables had been set out ten minutes ago, mother's work was not quite finished.

She was sitting close to the fender, with a blotting-pad on her knee, filling in cards for her first musical evening, as fast as her active little hand could scribble the names. She had been paying visits in the afternoon, and had not long exchanged the triple armour of her fashion-able visiting-gown for a picturesque arrangement of soft Indian silk, in which she could loll at ease in a chair that was as near the ground as a chair could be. Mother loved low seats; and Fritz loved to crawl over the back of mother's chair, and descend, an avalanche of boy, flaxen head down-wards, into mother's lap.

Fritz was the baby—not quite six years old—and allowed to do what he liked in mother's room and in mother's presence. In mother's absence he dropped from pet and plaything into the position of a troublesome little boy, who was openly spoken of by the household as a "young Turk, and spoilt by his mar till he was beyond bearing."

Stacie—the eldest—was at Elstree, and reported very highly of himself in the cricket-field ; but in the matter of lessons, as compared with certain saps and smugs among his schoolfellows, he owned to being "thick." He had visions of growing up to be a famous cricketer, invited all over England for the sake of his prowess in the field. Nor did he think ill of himself at the rougher sport of "footer," which occupied most of his thoughts in the winter terms.

Paul was educated at home by a morning governess, whom he hated ; not because she was unkind to him, but because it was a low thing for a boy to be taught by an old woman. Fritz had not yet achieved so much as a spelling acquaintance with the alphabet, in spite of all mechanical aid in the shape of ivory letters, picture-books, bricks, puzzles, and instructive games, and in defiance of the patient drudgery of a pale young person in the upper story, who was called a nursery governess, and treated like a nursemaid.

Of course the boys had nicknames. Eustace was Stacie. Paul was Poppy with his family, but with no one else; for he was one of those boys who are always more grown up than the grown-up people about them, and with whom the use of a pet name would seem an unwarrantable liberty. Fritz was Fluff—so named on account of curly hair which was in colour and texture like silkworm's silk, but which had been cut as short as Samson's before his fourth birthday.

"More 'vitations, mammy?" asked Fluff, sprawling on his stomach at his mother's feet while she wrote.

"Yes, darling."

"What a lot of parties you do give!"

"People are obliged to entertain, pet, if they go out as much as I do."

"To enter—— what?" inquired, Fluff, lifting up wondering blue eyes to the busy writer.

"To entertain—to give parties—you intelligent duck!" leaning down to kiss the top of his flaxen head and spilling some ink on her gown. "There, now see what you've made me do!"

"Oh, mammy, I didn't make you kiss me—you did it off your own bat."

The tea-things had been in the room a quarter of an hour. Stacie and Paul had been talking in a distant window, but a tempting odour of toasted bun having crept through the room, juvenile appetites were stimulated, and the two elder boys began to think it was time something should be done to draw mother's attention to their wants.

"Stacie," Paul began, "which do you like best, tea or ginger beer?"

"Ginger beer is the best after cricket; but I've heard that some people like tea at five o'clock in the afternoon," Stacie replied, rather loudly and distinctly.

After this audacity both the boys became explosive with smothered laughter; but Mrs. Lerwick went on scribbling, her pretty, fair head bending low over her blotting-pad, unconscious of this pointed dialogue.

"Well, there's one advantage about ginger beer,"

argued Stacie, a little louder than before. "A boy can run to the refreshment-tent and buy it for himself; but you can't run out into Palatine Square and buy a cup of tea."

This last indirect appeal aroused Mrs. Lerwick.

"Oh, you impatient creatures, in a hurry for your tea!"

"Not in a hurry, mums, but we like our tea best when it ain't quite cold."

"I haven't half finished my cards. You are such impatient children! Here is this darling Fluff as quiet as a lamb!"

She rose hastily, scattering a shower of cards and envelopes, and exposing the patient Fluff, who was lying on her silken train luxuriously devouring a large slice of pound cake.

"A perfect lamb!" exclaimed Stacie, pointing the finger of scorn. "That's the second piece. Pop and I have been watching him."

"And the only tea-gown I care for is all over crumbs and candied peel," protested Mrs. Lerwick.

"Fluff was so hungry," pleaded the youngest, his mouth stuffed with cake.

"My poor darling! Did his cruel mother keep him waiting? Come, boys. I am nearly fainting for want of my tea. But those cards have to be ready for the eight o'clock post."

The four sat crowding round the tea-table. Mother's low chair was particularly inconvenient for pouring out tea, but the boys helped her, and though there was a good deal of milk spilt in the tea-tray, they got on capitally. Cake, buns, bread-and-butter disappeared with astounding rapidity. Stacie and Pop told anecdotes—the elder of his masters at Elstree, the younger of base tricks played on his erudite and elderly governess.

Mother turned a smiling face to each, and tried to look as if she were listening intently; and, as she was expected only to listen, she was not found out.

Presently the boys began to ask questions.

"Where's father to-day?"

"Out of town," mother answered carelessly.

"But where?"

"Somewhere where there's racing. I think he had to go by the Great Northern."

"Newmarket, of course," said Stacie. "The Craven Meeting. Is he going to pull off anything this time?"

Mr. Lerwick was distinctly of the turf, turfy; and his eldest son might have heard more turf talk than is altogether good for a schoolboy.

"Oh! I've no idea," replied mother, absolutely indifferent. "His two-year-olds generally seem to lose."

"And so do his three-year-olds," said Stacie. "I'm ashamed of my name at Elstree when I find how little confidence any one has in my father's stable. Ward major groaned when he drew Madame Angot in our Leger sweep, for he knew the mare belonged to father."

"Oh, but he can't be always unlucky. I hope he will win the Derby this year."

"With Gasometer?" asked Paul.

"Or with Badmash. Badmash is the horse he believes in."

"Why, there's 25 to 1 offered against both of them," cried Eustace, contemptuously.

Mr. Lerwick's experiences on the turf heretofore

had not been cheerful. He had backed his own horses with gentlemanlike confidence in his own judgment and his own stable; and people knew that whatever Mr. Lerwick's horses were not, they were always "meant." His colours implied good faith, and a kind of careless honesty as of a man who could afford to lose.

It was popularly reported of Mr. Lerwick that his income was of such an expansive figure that he did not know how rich he was. He had inherited the chief interest in a great commercial house in the iron country, which had progressed by leaps and bounds under the new order of things in which success and failure are for the most part on a Titanic scale. It was supposed that his income flowed in upon him in a golden stream, whose force increased as the years rolled on. Let him spend as lavishly as he pleased—be as unlucky with his horses as hard Fate willed—he could never come to the end of the income produced by his share in Lerwick and Co. Here was no question of a Jubilee Plunger inheriting a quarter of a million. The wealth of Lerwick and Co. was an endless web of bank paper, of which no mind could conceive the exhaustion.

In order to assist him in the business of a life of pleasure, Anthony Lerwick had married one of the prettiest *débutantes* of her year—and, perhaps, also, one of the silliest; a fresh young beauty from Devonshire, launched in the choicest monied circles by a wealthy widowed aunt, and enjoying her first season as a butterfly enjoys his first flight among the roses. Ellinor Lerwick's admirers were all agreed that she was much too pretty to be clever, and they liked her better so, being for the most part golden youth, who had been more distinguished on the river than in the schools. She was quite intelligent enough for her husband, who would have been bored to death by a clever wife, and would have exiled himself for life in Central Africa rather than endure the companionship of a strong-minded woman. Of anything that could be called mind in a woman Tony had a dislike which was akin to absolute fear; indeed, from mind masculine as well as from mind feminine he shrank with

unconcealed aversion. The society he liked best
was to be found in the saddle-room, the gun-room,
his trainer's cottage, or among the blue-jackets
on his yacht. That a man should seek entertainment in the inside of a book seemed to him
as extraordinary as that a solitary prisoner should
make spiders or mice his companions. The things
he liked were the things he could see, touch,
and understand—horses, dogs, guns, boats. He
could not appreciate a joke that was not of the
practical kind. The men he liked were men of
his own calibre. The only woman he liked was
his wife.

As a husband, Tony Lerwick stood out from
the ruck—a first prize in the matrimonial lottery.
He admired his wife as much fourteen years
after marriage as he had admired his girlish
bride blushing under a cloud of tulle. In his
eyes those years had only made her lovelier.
She had not disappointed him as some of his
horses had done, by growing coarse instead of fine.
She had "furnished" just in the right degree; and
her figure, in acquiring a womanly plumpness,

had retained all the grace of her girlhood. His Nellie could do no wrong. She was the prettiest thoroughbred in his stables. She could not be too extravagant, too frivolous, too selfish to please him. All that she did, all that she said, found favour in those indulgent eyes.

Mrs. Lerwick went back to her nest by the fire and her batch of invitation cards ever so long before the boys had finished tea. The children's hour had resolved itself—so far as maternal companionship goes—into the children's ten minutes. Again the pretty fair head bent itself over the blotting-pad, and the busy pen scribbled and scampered along.

The boys went on chattering in low voices. They emptied the dish of toasted buns, about which there was more coagulated butter than a careful nurse would approve; but it was the nurse's hour as well as the children's hour, and the custodian of the little boys' health was at the bottom of the house gossiping over cups and saucers with the housekeeper and the French maid.

When the dishes and the teapot were empty, and there was a terrible mess in the tea-tray, Fluff suddenly wearied of the entertainment.

"May we go to the Surbiton and sail our boats, mummy?" he asked; but the pen rushed on, and he had to repeat the question several times in an ascending treble before it was answered.

The Surbiton was Fluff for Serpentine. Fluff had a prodigious command of the English tongue, but he was not particular about details, and proper names were often beyond his limits.

"No, darling, it is too late," came the tardy answer.

"No, it ain't too late!"

"Yes, loveliest, it will be dark in half an hour. You know you never go out after tea at this time of the year."

"That's Tommy rot!" cried Fluff.

The fair head started up with a jerk of horror, but reproof was addressed to the quarter where it is least expected.

"Eustace, this is your doing. You bring this horrid language from Elstree."

"If I do, it's useful to all of us," said Eustace, accustomed to have other people's sins laid upon his shoulders. "I heard you tell the Governor that the last novel you read was Tommy——"

"No, Eustace, not Tommy," interjected Paul, who was the most serious of the three, made grave beyond his years by the overshadowing of his governess's mature intellect. "Mother only said utter rot—not Tommy."

"I'm very sorry I ever used such a disgraceful word," exclaimed mother, and then concluded with withering emphasis, "or that I should have a son rude enough to remind me that I was capable of being vulgar."

Eustace jumped up from the tea-table with a vehemence that made the cups and saucers rattle.

"That's what always happens when Fluff does anything wrong," he said, marching to the door. "I get blamed for it."

He slammed the door behind him; and the doors in Palatine Square are solid six-panelled doors, the banging whereof resounds from basement to garret.

"What a temper!" sighed Mrs. Lerwick, despair-ingly. "He is becoming positively unmanage-able."

Such a little spurt of temper on Eustace's part was not an uncommon occurrence in Palatine Square; though at Elstree he was reckoned one of the best-tempered fellows in the school. Sooth to say, Mr. Lerwick's eldest son and heir did not get the best of it in the family circle. As the eldest, and as a schoolboy, he was supposed to be harder than his younger brothers, and his hard-ness was tested by a good many hard knocks. He had never pretended to be as clever as Paul— had always been willing to be the second, not the first—and had freely owned that at school he was called "thick," such thickness being taken to stand for intellectual inferiority. And so even Fluff learnt somehow to laugh at his eldest brother's deficiencies—or, at least, to laugh at Paul's jokes about them.

And yet what would those juniors have done without the schoolboy? Who was it taught them which of all the summer's cricket matches and all the winter's football matches were worth being excited about? Who was it told them the relative strength of Eton and Harrow—of Blackheath and Richmond? Why, Eustace, of course; for even that brilliant Tandy, past master of all turf knowledge, was no authority upon cricket, and scarcely knew the difference between Rugger and Socker, and, indeed, owned that he "took no stock" of either game.

What would their vocabulary have been like without Eustace? Mere nursery talk, the language of boys given over to the teaching of women. Without Eustace they would not have known that money was "oof," and that a boy who had half a crown a week pocket-money was an "oof-bird." Unenlightened by Eustace, they would have gone on talking about "sovereigns" instead of calling those useful coins "quids" or "thick 'uns;" nor would they ever have acquired the manly habit of terminating every noun substantive with the syllable -er. Tandy had been useful to them; but though Tandy was a young man of vast judgment, he lacked language, and expressed his deepest thoughts by a significant action of the eye and eyebrow, or a long low whistle, rather than by words.

Thus, had it not been for Eustace and those fresh breathings of boyish life that he brought from Elstree, Paul and Fluff might have talked like babies long after they were in trowsers.

Fluff had removed himself to the other end of the room, out of the path of the storm, and had taken all the silver toys off one of his mother's favourite tables, and was sitting on the floor making railway trains with them—a harpsichord, two armchairs, a bird-cage, a bedstead, a sofa—all hooked together and pushed along the velvet pile at express speed by Fluff's dexterous little hands.

"Miss Warren says you don't know how to manage any of us; I heard her tell Perry so," said Paul, who was seated luxuriously in a large armchair, brooding.

"Then she told Perry something that's not true,

and if Miss Warren indulges in insolent remarks about me she will be dismissed at the end of the quarter."

" I wish you would dismiss her, and let me go to Elstree with Eustace."

" Yes, and come home a coarse rough bear, like Eustace, thinking and talking of nothing but cricket."

" Well, I can't go on for ever learning of an old woman," groaned Paul. " I know more Latin than Eustace, and I'm a book further on in Euclid. Why shouldn't I go to Elstree next term ? "

" Because it's quite enough to have one schoolboy in the family," protested Mrs. Lerwick, who had allowed her sons to flutter her spirits considerably, so that it was all she could do to put her cards into the right envelopes, and manipulate the gold-handled stamp-damper without messing the thick " Royal Family " paper.

" I'm sure I sometimes wish you could have always remained babies," she murmured presently, when the last envelope was sealed.

" Perhaps you would have liked us never to

be born," said Paul. "That would have been still more convenient."

Tears sprang to the pretty blue eyes—those blue eyes which Fluff's so exactly matched—and Mrs. Lerwick started up in a little burst of wounded feeling.

"You are a heartless boy," she exclaimed. "Ever so much worse than your brother. He only slams doors ; you try to hurt one's feelings."

"Oh, dear!" groaned Paul. "I only answered your own remark. Look at Fluff. He's playing old gooseberry with your silver."

There was an exclamation, and a rustle of silken skirts across the floor. The toys were rescued, Fluff was slapped—a very small slap, which produced a very big squall. Electric bells were rung —bells that rang downstairs—bells that rang upstairs. Nursery governess and footman rushed to the rescue, and Fluff went off like Eugene Aram, between two sturdy custodians. Paul picked himself listlessly out of a nest of satin pillows and Japanese antimacassars, and moved slowly towards the door.

"When is the little Auntie coming again?" he asked.

"Not till we go back to Heatherside."

"And when will that be?"

"Why, not till the end of the season, child. We have only just come to town."

"Only just! It seems ages since we came! I hate London."

And thus without a word of farewell the last of the three departed to his own kingdom in the attics. Two had left in wrath and one in silence, and so ended the children's hour.

Pretty Mrs. Lerwick sat down on the carpet and picked up the silver toys one by one with a rueful visage. Delicate little corners were bent, the threads of the 'cello were broken, a leg of the harpsichord was doubled up, the airy, fairy roof of the bird-cage was squashed in on the tiny macaw that should swing below it.

"They are quite spoilt," sighed Ellinor Lerwick, "and I shall never get such pretty ones again until we go back to Genoa."

CHAPTER II.

HOW THE RICH LIVE.

EUSTACE went back to Elstree next day. He had come to Palatine Square for a day and a night, being wanted in Burlington Street by a gentleman whom he looked upon as one of the enemies of the human race—a very scientific and superior person, who did all sorts of disagreeable things to Eustace's mouth and teeth, ruthlessly extracting any tooth whose position offended his hypercritical eye. Bad as the extraction was, Eustace could bear that like a hero ; but worse remained behind, in the shape of what the dentist called "taking an impression," in which process hot red wax was crammed into his mouth and kept there till it cooled, at the risk of suffocation—the result of which ordeal by hot wax was a silver, or gold, or vulcanite plate, which made life more or less of a burden; while it was accounted basest villainy on the part of Eustace if he wore this modern instrument of torture in his pocket instead of on his jaws.

All the morning of his brief holiday had been devoted to this dreary business of having his teeth pulled out and his mouth modelled for another new plate—a plate which was to exercise the severest pressure upon two obstinate little tusks which the dentist talked of learnedly as canines. Nobody asked Eustace whether he thought the game was worth the candle, or whether he would not just as soon keep the canines as nature made them. He complained that he was handed over to Mr. Waytwright as if he had been a black slave.

" Has a fellow to wait till he is twenty-one before he has any property in his own mouth ? " Eustace asked at the breakfast-table in the schoolroom; but there was nobody present of sufficient learning to answer the question. " Can his parents have a sixth-form boy strapped into a chair and tortured ? "

"Oh, Stacie, you have never been strapped!" cried Fluff.

"No, but I expect it would come to that if I didn't give in," said Eustace, darkly.

"Becos if you was strapped," said Fluff, musingly, "I should like to be there to see."

Eustace had been huffed yesterday at tea, but the sun never went down on his wrath. His temper was quick, but his affections were warm and strong. He adored the pretty fair-haired mother; and as he had to leave home early, he pleaded for an interview in mother's bed-room.

She heard the voice in the corridor, and called out, "Stacie, Stacie darling," and he went into the bright room which opened out of mother's morning room, with three windows overlooking the branching limes and chestnuts in the square. He found her sitting up in bed in a blue silk *matinée*—a fair girlish face looking out of a nest of pale blue frilling and lace-trimmed pillows.

Mrs. Lerwick was sitting up to take her morning chocolate, while her French maid held a review of gowns, tippets, fichus, and other finery, discoursing vivaciously as she tossed the costly frippery about.

"But truly Madame has nothing to wear; this blue gown is altogether impossible."

"Oh! I am so fond of that blue surah—come and kiss me, Stacie—I must wear it again. It fits me better than anything Amelie has made for ages."

"But, Madame, have the goodness to look at the edge of the skirt—cut to pieces."

"When does your train go, love? But you can mend that hem, Babette."

Babette shrugged her lean little shoulders and threw down the blue silk frock as if it were almost too foul a thing to hold any longer in her superfine fingers.

"But, Madame, that soft silk does not mend itself—there is not enough of substance to hold a needle."

This meant that the blue frock was cashiered. Mrs. Lerwick would see it no more; but some-body else would go to Hampton Court in it next

Sunday afternoon, escorted by one of Mr. Hunter's under-cooks from the famous confectioner's on the other side of the square.

Stacie clambered on to a chair beside the bed, and gave his mother a vigorous hug.

"I hope you've enjoyed your holiday, dearest," she said, in the midst of a shower of kisses.

"I've enjoyed seeing you—I didn't enjoy the dentist."

"No, no, of course not. But I want all my sons to be handsome."

She looked for something on the littered table, where a fat, yellow-covered French novel, a mammoth silver eau-de-Cologne bottle, a fan, a heap of letters, three lace-edged handkerchiefs, and the chocolate service were crowded anyhow. She picked a lizard-skin purse out of the jumble, and opened it, and a shower of gold rolled over the silken coverlet.

"Oh, mummy, how rich you are!"

She gave Eustace a couple of sovereigns, and had to submit to a second hug, while Babette picked up the rest of the gold, and placed it in a little pile on the dressing-table with ostentatious carefulness.

"Won't I have a ripping bat," exclaimed Eustace, and a voice called from without—

"Now, Master Eustace, unless you want to lose your train."

"Why, of course I want to lose my train," he said, with a last kiss from the pretty mother, "but I mustn't do it," and off he ran.

"You can put out the pink crépon for Sandown," sighed Mrs. Lerwick as she picked up the yellow-backed novel and twirled the leaves listlessly.

Palatine Square, as everybody knows, is one of the choicest positions in West End London. It is an old-world square in which there are scarcely two houses exactly alike. Some have been rebuilt and are palaces, Italian, German, or Early English, with roofs that aspire sky-wards, minarets and watch-towers, campaniles and clustered chimneys, loggia and oriel windows, all that is fantastical and expensive in architecture. Other houses remain just as they were under the first and second George, when Palatine Square was young; houses so plain and homelike that one might fancy one's self in a country manorhouse. Again, there are a few much smaller houses—a cosy little bachelor house here and there, squeezed in between two colossal neighbours—houses with a rustic-looking balcony and verandah, and a delicate patrician grace in their modest stairways, and low-ceiled rooms opening one into the other, altogether suggestive of those good old times when there were meadows and rural lanes north of Palatine Square, and when the hangman's cart might be seen on the Oxford Road any morning, carrying its wretched burden to Tyburn.

Mr. Lerwick's house was one of the largest in the Square as to reception-rooms, and one of the worst as to bedrooms. It was an old house; and though it had been gorgeously decorated and furnished at Mr. Lerwick's expense, there had been no thought of putting on a new and higher roof, and letting light, space, and air into those terrible third-floor rooms.

Fascinated with the lofty double drawing-room, the six tall windows, the Italian chimney-pieces, Mrs. Lerwick had gone up to the top floor predisposed to be delighted with all she found there.

"Oh, Tony!" she exclaimed, as she and her husband went upstairs, "what a house for parties! We must have it."

"But they are asking thirty thousand for a forty-year lease."

"Is it much?"

"And the ground rent is a hundred and fifteen."

"That sounds very little. Those drawing-rooms, Tony! You must let *me* furnish those. You shall have your own way in all the rest of the house."

"But, Nell, I haven't made up my mind to buy it."

"But you will make up your mind I know, dear, when you've had another look at those drawing-rooms," pleaded his wife, and slim pearl-grey fingers twined themselves round Tony Lerwick's large doe-skin thumb.

They had newly returned from a winter's yacht-
ing in the Mediterranean, and had been house-
hunting for a week before an obsequious agent
brought them to Palatine Square to view—that
was the agent's expression—Lord Somebody's
house, only vacated at Christmas.

Mrs. Lerwick tripped lightly through the upper
rooms, holding her silken skirt off the dirty floors,
and looking about with a smiling casual air,
counting the rooms as she passed through, and
not happening to remark that there was hardly
an inch between the ceiling and the top of her
husband's hat.

"Eustace's bedroom," she said, pointing to a
little room at the back. "Such a dear tiny room—
I'll have it furnished so sweetly for him; all
bamboo, with rose-bud chintz curtains. The day
and night nurseries; lovely panelled walls, and
sweet old basket grates; and a double-bedded
room for nurse and Miss Perry."

"I thought a governess expected a room to
herself."

"Not Miss Perry. She is only a nursery

governess. One can't put up with airs from a person of that kind."

"No. But she mayn't be able to put up with no air," said Tony, dryly, "and I'll be hanged if she'll get much in such a dog-kennel as this, if you put two beds in it."

"Dog-kennel, Tony! With that lovely Adam mantelpiece!"

"Adam won't keep her cool in the dog days," muttered Tony.

But he was not strong enough either in argument or in will to oppose his pretty wife; so the lease of the fine house in Palatine Square was bought, and the last modish upholsterer—who called himself an artist—was let loose in the drawing-rooms, and Louis Seize and a chilly severity of line being the rage that year, the result was more adapted to the tropics than to the average English summer. Slim straight legs of chairs and tables reflected themselves in a polished floor as on the surface of deep water; the pale azure curtains fell in straight lines from the six tall windows. The rooms had a cold grandeur and bleak spaciousness that

frightened Fluff out of his baby wits if he
happened in his quest of "Mummy" to run in and
find only emptiness. He would make off as fast
as his little legs would carry him, leaving the great
half-door to swing .slowly and silently to on its
superior rising-butt hinges, as if some ghostly
hand had closed it.

Sooth to say, though no grisly legend attached
itself to that house in Palatine Square, there was
a feeling of ghosts in some of the rooms and
corridors which moved children, and even grown-
up servants, with sensations of vague fear. The
shadows hung so darkly in those low-ceiled
passages above. There were such strange closets
—closets within closets, doors within doors; a
ghostly back staircase which had been shut off at
the bottom of the second flight years and years
ago, and now only harboured mice and mustiness.

Even Mrs. Lerwick, proud as she was of her
drawing-rooms when her friends were grouped
about at stately distances after a dinner-party, or
at one of her concerts, when there was barely
standing room—even she confessed that the rooms

made her melancholy when there were no people. It may have been partly on this account that Mrs. Lerwick was seldom at home of an evening without people.

A London house, with a London mother, means a dull life for small boys, even if their shelties take them for an early gallop in the Row every fine morning, where they bucket along, much to the discomfiture of some of the elderly gentlemen in the Liver Brigade, who, jogging up and down quietly on their over-fed cobs, are apt to envy Herod his despotic power, or to regret the national neglect of Malthus.

" Pipe them kids ! " cries a gutter snipe, with bitter emphasis, as the two boys, dressed alike in neat little jackets and breeches, and drab gaiters, and billycock hats, trot along Prince Frederick Street on their way to the Park. But after a week of such morning rides the pampered Palatine Square children sicken at the monotonous exercise; and Paul informs his friend Tandy, the children's groom, that all riding except to hounds is Tommy rot. The fact that the morning ride is insisted

on as a matter of hygiene naturally takes all the
flavour of pleasantness out of it. In Dorsetshire they are keen enough, for even when there
are no hounds afoot, the furze bushes on those
breezy commons, the ditches that divide the fields,
afford ample scope for " lepping," to say nothing
of a certain rural course where they can race their
ponies while the dew is on the summer grass, and
while the keen morning air in their shelties' nostrils
quickens the pace and stimulates to skittishness.

In London, Paul complains there is nothing to
do. Even the theatres to which mother takes
them from time to time offer but feeble joys—
Tommy rot, in the shape of serious plays and
sentimental comedy, being the dramatic staple
at the fashionable houses, and burlesque the rare
exception—save in the unpalatable form of comic
opera, where the fun is swamped by the music.

If father would take them to the music halls
there might be something to live for ; but father
has pledged himself not to take them, by a solemn
promise to mother, whose lamentable ignorance is
allied to ridiculous prejudices, and who believes

every music hall to be a sink of iniquity, where wicked songs are sung to wicked people.

"I hate the London season," exclaims Paul, with his shoulders sunk into the padded angle of a large armchair, and his navy blue legs swinging in space. "It's simply beastly!"

"You might have better reason for saying that if you lived in the slums at the back of the mews," his governess answers gravely.

"No, I shouldn't, for I should have something to *amuse* me," says Paul with a tremendous emphasis upon the pun, of which Miss Warren takes not the faintest notice. "I could keep rabbits—I could go into the stables whenever I liked."

"How would you like sleeping eight in a room?"

"Can't say! I never tried it."

Miss Warren sighs, but her rule with boys of Paul's stamp is to ignore impertinence. He has never been able to sting her to retort or argument. If Minerva herself had condescended to be his mentor that divine lady could not have held herself more aloof from the little world of his

small mind.   He never has had the satisfaction
of knowing what she thinks of him.   Miss
Warren is nearer forty than thirty.   She is grave
and pale, a neat thin figure always appropriately
dressed.   No salient point in her physiognomy
or her attire lends itself to juvenile laughter.   She
wears no foolish feathered hat, carries no prepos-
terous parasol or gampish umbrella.   Her garments
are neither old-fashioned nor new-fashioned, but
of a severe simplicity that bears the stamp of a
tailor who knows how the world is moving.

Paul did not love his governess, but he could
not help respecting her, and he could not help
learning of her, and, worse, as he thought, could
not help being interested in his work with her ;
for she made him think as well as learn, and his
young mind grew under her teaching.   She had
read a good deal, for a woman, and when compared with the elegant Mrs. Lerwick, who had
forgotten all she had ever learnt in the schoolroom, Miss Warren seemed an inexhaustible
well-spring of knowledge.

But then Miss Warren laboured under the disadvantage of being what Paul's particular friend Tandy, the groom, called "a plain-headed one." "I see your new governess this morning, Master Paul," said Tandy, "and she *is* a plain-headed one!" And Miss Warren laboured under the disadvantage of not liking dogs—in the house.

"If she don't like 'em in the house, Master Paul, you bet she don't like 'em nowheres. I knows the kind of people as likes a dog in his place—and that dog's place, in them people's estimation, is the bottom of the river."

Miss Warren, not liking dogs, was at once put down as a person of evil instincts and concealed vices—such as cruelty and treachery ; and it was a disconcerting thing to discover that mother's Spitz insisted upon adoring Miss Warren, and that Fluff's fox terrier, Pincher, had never been known to growl at her.

"Spitz never had much intellect," said Paul. "His brains have all run to hair—but I didn't know that Pincher was little better than a fool."

Nobody in Palatine Square knew that in her

small way Miss Warren was a philanthropist, and
that much of her afternoon leisure was spent in
the slums of West End London—the insanitary
hovels that lie hidden behind the stately streets
of the Palatine Hill, and for which the strong
hand of improvement waits, armed with a pickaxe, to lay them all low when the leases run
out. And when that day of annihilation comes,
the little laundress, the cobbler, the servants'
dressmaker, the jobbing tailor, the charwoman,
and the professional beggar, will have to carry
their rags and their sticks, their measles and
scarlet fever far away from the Palatine neighbourhood, and the only shadow across the sunshine of its splendour will vanish away.

Yes, Paul respected his governess, although
she never called him Poppy, or Paulino, as his
mother did, or Poll, or Polly, as his easy-going,
good-natured father loved to call him. He had
made up his mind not to like her; and he was
a young person with a strong will and a resolute
temper that had been fostered by eleven years
of having his own way. No, Paul was not

plastic. Two years ago, when he was handed over to Miss Warren, he had wanted to go to Elstree, and not to have a governess. And after that could he be expected to like his governess? It was not Miss Warren's fault but her misfortune that he must needs detest her to the end of their acquaintance. He couldn't help getting on under her tuition. She was so beastly conscientious. Everybody except himself was pleased with the arrangement, and Elstree and its cricket field were further off than ever.

"He is ever so much cleverer than Stacie," said his mother. "Awfully advanced for eleven years old. He knows more Shakespeare than I do."

Paul remarked that this was easy, as dear Mummy's ideas about Hamlet, Othello, Macbeth, and Lear were somewhat mixed.

"I believe if I told her that Hamlet smothered his wife, or that Macbeth's wicked daughters turned him out-of-doors in a thunderstorm, she wouldn't know I was greening her," said Paul.

Even Tandy, the groom, had been forced to

admit that Miss Warren was a person of vast learning.

" I never see such a pig for books, Master Paul," said Tandy, " she regular eats 'em. I meets her on the common when I'm exercisin' in Dosset, and she's allus got her nose in a book. Trudges along readin', readin', readin'. I wonder she don't let herself down on her knees over them hillocks."

One redeeming virtue Miss Warren had, and it was a great one. She did not live in the house. She came at nine o'clock—with a most odious regularity—and she was supposed to leave at one. But she was reprehensibly lax in the matter of departure, and had sometimes committed the in-justice of staying till a quarter past, in spite of clocks, and the broadest hints from her pupil. Neither in London nor in Dorsetshire did she take bite or sup under her employer's roof, save when— once in six months or so—formally invited to tea, to meet the curate and his wife, or Mr. Lerwick's land steward and his daughter. She was liberally paid, and the engagement suited her. In London she lived with her people in a back street at

Brompton. In Dorsetshire she boarded with the village doctor's family, and helped the doctor by nursing his poorest patients.

A London Spring, a London house, and all the restrictions of a London life had begun to show their deteriorating effect in pale cheeks and languid limbs before May began ; and even Mrs. Lerwick's pretty eyes, which had so many pretty things to look at, observed that Fluffy had not quite such a nice colour as he had had at Heatherside, where he played about in the open air all day long. Paul was always headachy in town ; but that was put down to his superior intellect, and never to want of oxygen. Fluff's pallor was considered more alarming, and the family doctor was consulted, who prescribed a tonic and plenty of outdoor exercise; advice which caused a good deal of ill-will and a good many tears on the part of the patient, who preferred his corner of the nursery floor and his tin soldiers and clockwork locomotives to the parks or the square. Indeed, it was one of the young mother's grievances that her darling preferred the stuffiest corner in that stuffy room—with the treasures of the toy cupboard—to the elegant luxury of her Victoria, and could only be induced by bribery to accompany her in her afternoon drive.

"I hate going for a drive," he grumbled, when his mother sent him off to be dressed in his newest velvet suit for one of these afternoon airings.

" Oh, Fluff, hate going out with me ? "

"I ain't with you much of the time.   You're sticking in some shop, and I have to sit outside ; and dirty-looking beggars come and worry ; and you won't let me have Pincher to bark at them."

"Of course I must do my shopping ; but you are in the open air, and that's what the doctor wishes.   You ought to enjoy the drive in the Park afterwards."

"I don't call that a drive—crawling along—for you to keep bowing and grinning at people, or standing still for young fellows to talk to you ; and you won't let me talk to the footman."

"Certainly not.   No well-behaved little boy would want to talk to a servant in public."

"That's stuck-up nonsense!" said Fluff, in an ascending scale of naughtiness, which ends in his being sent to St. James's Park with his nursery governess, in deep disgrace, but with a basket of bread to feed the ducks, and half a crown to buy a toy boat.

CHAPTER III.

FOR THE BLUE RIBBON.

THOSE London days are so colourless and dull. One sultry May morning Fluff's languid legs become a burden too heavy to be borne, and he informs his mother that he wishes he were dead, while poor Miss Perry's reddened eyelids and obvious depression indicate trouble.

On being closely questioned Miss Perry confesses that Fritz has been more than usually naughty that morning; that he kicked her under the table all through breakfast, and that he obstinately refused even to look at his B.A. Ba book. Upon which pretty Mrs. Lerwick loses all patience with Miss Perry.

"You haven't the least idea of managing a child. You ought to be a dressmaker's apprentice," she says pettishly, and then tries her hand at managing Fluff by boxing his ears sharply, and carrying him roaring down to her morning room, where she gives him chocolate creams.

It may be that Mrs. Lerwick herself is a little overstrung this morning; for this is the last Wednesday in May, a day of days; and she is going to Epsom in a new frock for the ninth time in her married life, to see her husband lose the Derby.

Eight times has that devoted patron of the turf tried for the blue ribbon—and eight times has hope told its flattering tale only to end in disappointment. Tony tells himself that the late Mr. Merry tried and failed almost as many times before the canary jacket flashed past the winning post in front of all competitors. He reminds himself of Robert Bruce and the spider. He says again and again: "It's dogged as does it." And dogged he means to be till the race is won.

Fluff sprawls on his mother's favourite sofa, kicking about his mother's prettiest satin pillows, and sobbing in a subdued diminuendo as the chocolate creams melt in his mouth, and make little brown streaks at the corners of his pale lips. Mrs. Lerwick walks about in an agitated way; goes to her bedroom to look at the new frock which Babette has spread out for her admiration—one of those simple little frocks of China silk, Indian muslin, and French lace, which cost people in Palatine Square thirty guineas or so, and look hardly worth five; but the highest merit in frocks is that they should look like cheap simplicity and cost a great deal.

She stands before the new frock musingly— hardly seeing that dainty vision of mauve muslin, white silk and Valenciennes—haunted by Fluff's face.

"It would be such a treat for them," she says to herself. "Why not?"

Mr. Lerwick looks in from his dressing-room.

"Fit as a fiddle!" he cries, waving a telegram. "We shall pull it off this time, Nellie; and if he wins——"

" "You'll give me those sapphires?"

"Yes, Nell, anything you like!"

"Fluff is not very well this morning, dear. Would you mind the boys going with us? They have never seen a really big race—and there would be plenty of room on the coach."

"Mind? No, of course not! Let the little beggars come," Lerwick answers, carelessly. "Let them see their father's horse win in a canter. It will be something for them to remember when they are men and have stables of their own."

"And you really think this one will win?" questions his wife, with a faint sigh.

"Think? It's a certainty!"

"But he's not the favourite."

"So much the better for us, Nell. I've kept him as dark as I could—but the knowing ones have smelt out that it's a sure thing."

The two boys were enraptured when mother announced the good news. Paul threw Kennedy's Latin Grammar up to the ceiling in the very midst of a deponent verb, and dismissed Miss Warren with a grand air. Fluff accepted the ordeal of washing and dressing with smiles and good temper, and allowed Miss Perry to lace his boots without any disagreeable remarks about her clumsiness or the warmth of her poor little industrious hands, or the untidiness of her hair.

At half-past eleven father's coach was at the door, and the boys were upon it, perched just behind the driving-box, ready for the start, though all the rest of the party were in the drawing-room talking to mother. The wine-baskets and food-baskets, and wraps and sun-umbrellas, and a great bunch of La France roses which some-body had brought for mother, had all been put inside the coach, where a couple of footmen were to sit in charge of them. Paul and Fritz waited impatiently for the other people, afraid that mother's usual unpunctuality would make them late for the great race, till Tandy told them there was "no fear." Tandy was to sit behind with another groom, who in livery looked his twin brother, but in stable clothes wasn't a bit like him.

At last the smart women, mother's friends,

were handed up to their seats, some tripping lightly up the ladder, but two of the elder ladies somewhat fussy and nervous, to Fluff's secret amusement. And then father and his friends, who had stopped in the dining-room for a brandy and soda, clambered into their places, and father gathered the reins into his doeskin palm, and the coach moved off, while Tandy and his twin sprang lightly up at the back, and the "yard of tin" rang out over Palatine Square in a triumphant blast blown by Colonel Pamby, father's favourite chum, who was a famous performer.

What a delightful journey it was in the bright May sunshine and the fresh west wind. Mother and her friends complained of the dust, and objected because scraps of straw and London dirt were blown in their faces as they crossed the bridge by the Houses of Parliament—but women always find something to grumble about, Paul told Fluff in a whisper.

Colonel Pamby was a delightful companion on a coach. He announced the names of all the great buildings they passed, always wrong; and

E

told the ladies the most ridiculous stories about everything, winking at Paul and letting him into the joke, as if he had been a grown man. He kissed his hand to maid-servants looking out of upper windows; he startled quiet people upon the pavement in the Clapham Road by hailing them as old acquaintances, asking particular questions about their relations—whether Maria's rheumatism was better or Uncle Nick had recovered from the gout? And when the victim —some guileless elderly lady, perhaps—looked up with bewildered countenance, Colonel Pamby blew one of his mighty blasts upon the yard of tin, as the coach rolled on and left the victim a quarter of a mile behind before she had time to think.

Father was a famous whip—indeed, it was the one thing which he was supposed to do best in the world; and except when they almost drove over a nurse and perambulator near Kennington Park, neither Paul nor Fluff had any fear, though the fine team of upstanding browns seemed to devour the road between Kennington and

Mitcham. At Mitcham they had a fresh team —grays and chestnuts—which had been sent on over-night, so they drove on to the downs in spanking style; and they felt that every eye was upon them; eyes that admired and envied, as father steered the coach cleverly into the place that had been engaged for it.

"I know what you want, boys," cried Colonel Pamby, in his strong, jovial voice; "you want a brandy and soda to wash down the dust."

Mother gave a little scream of horror at this remark, not understanding that it was only the Colonel's facetious way of saying that *he* wanted a brandy and soda. The footmen opened a couple of baskets in a twinkling, while the grooms were leading the horses away and drinks were handed about — tiny *foie-gras* sandwiches, and glasses of champagne which the ladies sipped daintily and gave back to the servants more than half full, while they looked about them to see whether any of their smart friends were on the other coaches; and gipsy children crawled about the grass like insects, and gipsy mothers, with infants in their arms, begged for a chicken or a lobster for the baby, peering into half-open baskets with hungry eyes.

Mr. Lerwick and Colonel Pamby went off to the paddock together. The other gentlemen strolled away along the line of drags and carriages, and were lost in the crowd. The boys asked their father if they might go with him to see Badmash, and being somewhat curtly refused, they found life hardly worth living. Fluff did not conceal his disgust. The coach had been delightful as long as it was moving; but to sit on the top of a horseless vehicle, looking at the crowd, and the downs, and the sky, was not enough for pleasure.

Paul began to climb down, when his mother stopped him.

" You are to stay with us, Poppino."

" Us ! Who's us ? All the men are gone."

" But you are not a man."

" No, but I ain't blind. I want to walk about and have a look at things—and so does Fluff."

" Yes, yes, mummy, I'm tired of being up here."

"Oh, you naughty boys, when father is giving you such a delightful treat."

"It ain't a treat to be up here among a lot of women," grumbled Paul. "If it is, why don't Colonel Pamby and the governor stop?"

"How dare you talk of the 'governor?'"

"Oh, you want boys to be spoons, and say papa' like a doll with a phonograph in its stomach," retorted Paul, in open mutiny. "I want to go to the paddock and see if Badmash looks like winning—or, if I mayn't go there, I can stroll about the course and look up my friends."

"I won't allow you to leave the coach. You would be going about among the ragged children and getting scarlet fever. Look, there's a dog on the course. The race is going to begin."

"And there's a bobby chasing him!" cried Fluff.

The dog made a diversion, and it was fun to see the mounted constables riding gallantly up and down, and a close line of blue-coats thrusting the crowd back on either side, till the long strip of

sward lay clear and smooth like a green ribbon.
And then came the race before the Derby; and
eleven horses in whose fortunes the bookmakers
seemed the only people interested, distinguished or
disgraced themselves after the manner of horseflesh.   And when that race was over, Mr. Lerwick
came back to the coach flushed and feverish,
laughing and talking more than usual; and more
bottles of the last fashionable champagne were
opened; indeed, Paul, watching his father keenly,
noted with a strange childish fear that the owner
of Badmash was drinking nearly all the time
between that preliminary race and the event of
the day.

Fluff, less thoughtful, but as observant, remarked upon the fact. "What a lot of champagne father drinks.   Isn't it bad for him,
mummy?"

"It won't hurt him to-day, dear. He only takes
it because he's anxious about the horse."

"But Badmash will win, won't he?   Father
said we were to see him win."

"I hope you will, dear. But horses are so

uncertain. They never seem to know their own minds," answered mother uneasily, and then she clasped the big doeskin paw with her delicate little hand. "Tony, he's going to win, ain't he?"

"God knows. There's a dead set against him in the ring. The bookies will be hit hard, and I shall make a pot of money, if he wins."

"Do they give you your money in a pot?" asked Fluff. "What kind of pot?"

But Anthony Lerwick was too preoccupied to answer infantine questions. That bottle of champagne had left him pale as ashes—and even Pamby the facetious was strangly silent, after his seventh brandy and soda, and only muttered little jocosities to Mrs. Lerwick to keep up her spirits. Mr. Lerwick had only come to the coach to speak to his wife, and for a glass of that particular brand which he had been told was the only wine worth drinking. He went back to the paddock with Pamby, to catch the last word of hope from his trainer, to see his jockey weigh-out and mount, to hang about horse and rider till the last moment, when they passed out of the gate—the jockey with sharp features set in a business-like gravity, the horse with every muscle quivering, on fire with impatience.

Poor Tony! He had tried so often for this prize, had backed his own horses with such un-flinching faith in trainer and jockey, and nothing but ill-luck had been his portion. He had never taken the trouble to reckon how much his racing stud and his book—that fatal book which was but a register of mistaken opinions—had cost him. A man who doesn't know how rich he is need not keep any account of his losses; but he knew roughly that he had been losing a good many thousands a year ever since he went on the turf. He didn't mind about the money. It mattered little whether he drew more or less any year from Lerwick and Co. A business on so gigantic a scale must be unaffected by private expenditure. What he felt was the disappointment, the humilia-tion, the shame of failing where other men succeeded.

No horse could have looked finer in the

preliminary canter.   Mrs. Lerwick devoured the animal with her eyes as he bounded along, seeming scarcely to touch the ground.   His light bay coat shone like golden-brown satin, and the mauve and white—her choice—were the prettiest colours on the course.   White jacket and mauve sleeves ; mauve and white cap.

"It's much prettier than if the jacket was mauve and the sleeves white, isn't it, Polo?" she asked, standing up on the seat, a white fluttering figure, with one hand on Paul's shoulder, and the other resting lightly on Fluff's head.

The flag fell—the horses were off with a sound like thunder.   The course was as hard as iron, and Badmash was a heavy horse who would have had a better chance on heavier ground.   The favourite was light as a sylph—fine as gold wire. The great seething crowd of London let loose for a holiday seemed to breathe as one man, and that man was holding his breath.   One minute of hope, half a minute of doubt, half a minute of despondency, and then—fifteen seconds of blank despair, and there rose that roar of unanimous voices which acclaims the triumph of the favourite.

It seemed a very long time before Tony and his friend came back, and Mrs. Lerwick sat silent, and feeling a sickness of despair, while the foot-men were serving luncheon—taking it upon them-selves to begin somewhat officiously as she thought —and while her friends were eating and drinking and chattering with an utterly heartless vivacity.

Of course they knew that with people of the Lerwicks' wealth, it was not a case for pity. But still it was provoking to go on losing a great race year after year. It must make them almost objects of ridicule. And she could not now with any grace ask Tony to buy her those sapphires, the finest set in London, the property of a gambling countess, who was blazing about London in paste duplicates of diamonds that had been sold.

Tony came back at last, looking as he did one day when his wife and children met him at Folke-stone, and he had just come off the boat after a stormy crossing.

"Has Badmash lost again?" Fluff asked dolefully.

"Not again, my laddie. This is the gee's first achievement on this particular course," answered Pamby, who could not be expected to share his friend's depression, not having adventured so much as a solitary sovereign upon Mr. Lerwick's horse. "His first and last appearance in this particular race."

"But father lost the Derby last year."

"Yes, Fluff, but with another horse. It takes a fresh 'un every time."

"Badmash is a beast," exclaimed Fluff, with vehement indignation.

"And I shan't have my sapphires," sighed pretty Mrs. Lerwick, and then with a little gush of affection, she slipped her hand under her husband's arm. He had mounted to the seat at her side, and was staring straight before him with a gloomy countenance.

"I hope you don't feel disappointed, Tony?"

"I oughtn't to. I'm used to it," he answered with a bitter lightness.

"I wish you'd sell all those horrid horses and sack your trainer," she said coaxingly.

Of course when one is ridiculously rich, spending a little more or less can't matter; but still, to Mrs. Lerwick's feminine judgment that training stable, with horses that never won a race, seemed a sad waste of money. There was a villa near Lecco to be sold last September when they were at Bellaggio, and she would have liked Tony to buy it. The price sounded a great deal in lire, but the villa would hardly have cost as much as that stupid stable—and it would be chic to own an Italian villa on the loveliest lake in Italy, even if one seldom had leisure to live in it.

CHAPTER IV.

A CLOUD OF FEAR.

THERE were no more treats after the Derby Day. The London season was now at its flood tide, and mother was going to parties every night. The night upon which she was due at only one party was an exception to the general rule of dinner and concert and dance, of " looking in " at this great house, and " going on " to another. She was always having new frocks. Fluff knew, for he was often called into her room to look at something especially pretty, and when he admired a frock or a mantle with enthusiasm he was said to have very good taste, to be altogether in advance of his years. Or if with infantine candour he called a frock ugly he was laughed at gaily, as a baby who knew no better.

"Why, it's the very height of the fashion, pet!" protested Mrs. Lerwick.

"Is it? Then I should like something lower down."

Paul was not consulted. He had been found unsympathetic, brusque almost to clownishness. He wondered why his mother had so many gowns; talked about "you women," and ".the money you chuck away on trumpery," as if he were a political economist.

A boy of that kind could hardly be petted by a pretty young mother like Mrs. Lerwick. Fluff would sit on the floor and turn over her jewels in their velvet nests, and choose the diamond necklace he was to have for his wife when he grew up and married.

"Father must have heaps of money to buy you all these," exclaimed Fluff; "or had you any of them before you were married?"

"No; girls don't have diamonds."

"Don't they? Not even rich girls?"

"Not even rich girls. It isn't good style."

"Were you a rich girl?"

" No—not exactly rich."

" Not rich like you are now ? "—searchingly.

" No."

" Were you poor ? "

" Of course not. How can you ask such silly questions ? "

" Little Auntie doesn't look as if she were rich."

" No, because she lives in the country, and doesn't go to parties, and doesn't want smart clothes."

" Doesn't she like pretty things ? "

" She couldn't wear them in a Devonshire village—where your grandfather lives."

Fluff asked a good many more questions. He had a thirst for information that afternoon. Why didn't Mother have Auntie to live at Palatine Square, and give her pretty frocks, and take her to parties—and then perhaps she would marry a rich man, like father ? On which his mother checked him indignantly, and told him it was very vulgar to talk of people's money.

" That is the way servants talk ! " she said.

" Yes, it is," assented Fluff; " they talk of you—

and father's money; and the maids say that you are both 'stravagant enough to run through your fortune if it was three times as much."

"Do they say that—to you?"

"No, but I hear them. I listened at the door yesterday when Sarah and Loo were cleaning the schoolroom."

"Insolent wretches! But you mustn't listen, Fluff. It's low and vulgar to listen. Only underbred little boys listen. Did you hear any more?"

"Loo said you're not so pretty as you was a year or two ago."

"Not you 'was,' Fluff—as you 'were.'"

"Loo said you didn't wear well."

"Loo! You must never call a servant Loo. I can't think where you get such vulgar ways."

"Sarah calls her Loo. And father calls you Nell."

"That's quite different. People of the same class may call each other what they like."

And then Mrs. Lerwick, in her light way, tried to explain to him the great gulf there was between a little boy who lived in Palatine Square, and the servants who waited upon him. She did not go quite so far as to say that the Creator had made them of a different clay ; but she tried to make him understand that they were always to be treated as creatures of a different race, with whom he could have no thoughts or feelings in common.

"It always distresses me to see your familiarity with Tandy," she said. "But while you are small and he has to ride by your side, I suppose that can't be helped. When you are big enough to manage your pony, Tandy will ride behind you."

"I'm not afraid of my pony ; but if Tandy rides behind me, who shall I have to talk to ?"

"Your brother, of course."

"Paul's so ignorant. Tandy knows everything —all about horses, and dogs, and rats, and birds —and everything. Tandy lived with a country doctor "—here Fluff sank his voice to a solemn whisper—"who kept fighting-cocks—and they fought ; and Tandy used to hold one, and the doctor held the other, and they were 'game' to

F

the last feather!" concluded Fluff, in a burst of enthusiasm.

"If I had known that of Tandy he should never have been engaged in our stable."

"Oh, come now, the stable's father's p'ovince— I heard him tell you so once when you grumbled at his horses always losing. The stable's his p'ovince. What is a p'ovince?"

It was a glorious summer. There was hardly a rainy day between Epsom and Goodwood. Ascot was a Saturnalia of hot weather and smart frocks and society babble. Mr. and Mrs. Lerwick hired a house at Windlesham for the race-week—a "place" in a park, where there was a pond that offered a secluded refuge for any unlucky member of the Jockey Club.

The place at Windlesham was roomy enough for a large house-party, but not large enough to accommodate Paul and Fritz and their belongings.

"Besides," said Mrs. Lerwick, during one of her rare visits to the schoolroom, as if continuing a line of argument, "it would be a pity to interrupt

Paul's studies when he is getting on so well with you."

She looked at Miss Warren for assent and encouragement; but that lady, who was always more provoking than anybody else in the world, chose to take an opposite view.

"I am generally sorry for any break in Paul's studies," she said gravely, "but I think in this hot weather the change to the country would do him and his brother worlds of good. If you did not care for me to run down by rail every day, I could lodge at a cottage in the neighbourhood, so that there need be no break in Paul's lessons."

Mrs. Lerwick — who had never liked Miss Warren—looked upon this proposal as an artful attempt of the daily governess to get herself included in the Ascot party.

"You forget that every cottage is let for the race-week, and that the Ascot trains are absolutely impossible," she answered pettishly.

"Then I could give Paul a holiday task, and he could send me his Latin exercise and his Euclid every day."

"It's absurd to talk like that when there is no room at Windlesham for the boys and their nurse."

"If you had said so in the first instance, Mrs. Lerwick, I should not have talked absurdly."

"My husband always invites too many people," grumbled Mrs. Lerwick, as if she were called upon to justify herself. "My own particular friends will be horridly squeezed. The only comfort is that in this delicious weather we shall almost live in the grounds, and those are too lovely."

Little as the two boys saw of father or mother in the London season, the week their parents spent at Ascot seemed cruelly long and dull; and the ghosts had it all their own way in Palatine Square. The staircase—the landings—the windows—were full of ghosts in the lingering June twilight—in those still hours when London was dining, and there were no sounds of carriage wheels in the square, and when the roar of the Palatine Hill was subdued to a distant murmur that might have been the summer sea. The silent house, from which all the servants except one kitchen wench

and a boot-boy had fled to their evening amuse-
ments—echoed with phantom footsteps. The very
air was full of ghosts—or the feeling of ghosts,
which was worse than the actual thing, Paul
thought, since it included such hideous possibilities.
Miss Perry had given him a little book of ghost
and goblin stories, translated from the German—
a fat, close-printed duodecimo—and from that
book of grisly horrors Paul had peopled the house
in Palatine Square. He loved the book—indeed,
books could not be too grisly for his liking—and
after such strong meat he bored himself with "Tom
Brown," or "Jackanapes," or the story of the boy
who was "misunderstood."

"I don't want to read about boys like myself,"
said Paul. "I'm misunderstood. I like something
that makes my hair stand up on end—or would, if
I was in a funk."

In the June twilight, when the deserted offices
and servants' hall testified to the willingness of the
ancillary mice to take the uttermost advantage of
the absence—to spend the afternoon at Putney
with a married daughter—of the housekeeper-cat

Paul *was* in a funk; for then the fiends, and midnight hearses, and shadowless men, and doppelgangers, and skeletons dragging their clanking chains, and vampires gorged with human blood, came out of the little fat book of German stories, and waited for him in every shadowy angle of the stairs. He could not see them; but he knew they were there. The empty rooms and closed doors—that sense of spaciousness and solitude—appalled him. He passed shuddering by his father's room on the half-flight, a fine room built out at the back, over the offices, with a wide old-world window, from which Mr. Lerwick could look into his stable yard, and even talk to the grooms. It was a cheery room when father was at home, and people were talking there, and passing in and out, and Colonel Pamby's full baritone voice and boisterous laugh echoed along the stone landing; but it was a place of nameless fears now when there was nothing but silence and solitude behind the closed door.

Paul paused one evening with his hand on the door-handle, wanting to go in and peep about, but afraid lest he should see his father sitting there in the twilight—the spectral likeness of his father, who was away at Windlesham.

And there was no electric light on that awful silent staircase—no friendly light to be turned on at the touch of a button. Mrs. Lerwick objected to the electric light, because it was cold, and garish, and—unbecoming. There were only inaccessible gas-lamps which that odious young man, an under footman, would not come and light until the house was pitch dark. No! He was in the stables enjoying himself. A loud burst of vulgar laughter rang up from the mews to the open window on the back staircase now and then; but there was nothing human in the sound—it was like the laughter of those German fiends.

Upstairs in the schoolroom Miss Perry sat by a window poring over a scrap of fancy work. Fritz had been in bed an hour, and Paul was enjoying the privilege of his superior years, and sitting up till nine.

"Are there no candles?" he asked despairingly, looking round the low dark room.

"Not an inch of candle. I've rung the bell till I am tired," wailed Miss Perry. "I don't believe there's a human being in the bottom of the house —unless it's burglars."

Pittman, the middle-aged nurse, had proved her confidence in Miss Perry by going visiting three evenings out of four during the Ascot week ; but she had generously suggested that Miss Perry should treat herself to a little outing on the fourth and last evening. She had friends in London, no doubt, who would take her to a theatre.

Yes, she had an aunt, a widow in comfortable circumstances, who would give her some kind of treat, if she were free to accept it ; and this being so, Pittman did not rest till Miss Perry had settled all about her evening out, which was to be to-morrow, Friday. Mr. and Mrs. Lerwick were expected home on Saturday. The gates of the Windlesham Paradise would close with the end of the week. Beauty, fashion, rank, and wealth would fade away like the figures in a diorama.

"I'll make those beastly servants hear," said Paul, pressing his finger on the button, and keeping it there while the electric bell trilled shrilly through the big empty house.

He had been holding his finger on the button for five minutes before the kitchen-drab appeared, breathless and indignant.

"Where are the candles?" roared Paul. "It's disgusting the way you beasts of servants behave when your master and mistress are away."

He felt there was manhood in this remonstrance, but he knew that he would not have dared to say as much to the butler, who would have withered him with imperial scorn, or to the under footman, who would have chaffed him, which would have been even more humiliating.

The kitchen-wench was surly, and told him that she didn't know why there was no candles, and it wasn't her work to look after the schoolroom candles. It was the third housemaid's work to clean the rooms. It was Thomas's place to wait upon the young gentlemen.

"And are Miss Perry and I to be left in the dark because Thomas chooses to go out, you low beast?" demanded Paul, feeling that this was a fit occasion upon which to assert himself. "Go and get some candles instantly."

To which the resentful kitchen-slut muttered that she didn't know where the candles "was kep'," and that it wasn't her work "to look for no candles."

"I should like to know what work you are fit for, you idle beggar," ejaculated Paul, while Miss Perry, standing by, kept meekly murmuring—

"Paul dear, don't be so rude."

"Vegetables—them's my work," said the girl, sturdily.

"Then go back to your vegetables, you incorrigible slut. I'd rather sit in the dark than be waited on by such a low creature," said Paul, who had heard a manly step upon the stair, and the footman Thomas whistling a music-hall melody.

The girl retreated, sullenly muttering, and a bright light flashed into the schoolroom from the landing outside.

"Come, Thomas," remonstrated Paul, as the man came in with his gas-taper, "don't you think it's rather rough upon us, your stopping out all the evening?"

"I didn't expect you'd want anything, Mr. Paul," the footman answered carelessly. "The house ain't hardly bearable downstairs on such a 'ot night."

"You might remember that all the other men are at Ascot."

"I do, and I wish I was there along of 'em," said Thomas; and then he took up the music-hall melody at the second part of the tune, and lighted the gas, turning up the three burners to their fullest power, at the risk of smoking the low ceiling.

Paul would like to have reproved him for whistling on duty, but didn't feel equal to it.

"I should infinitely prefer candles this hot weather," he said discontentedly.

"The housekeeper says there's to be no more candles burnt in the schoolroom."

CHAPTER V.

TÊTE DE LINOTTE.

SELDOM had there been such a delightful summer.
Mrs. Lerwick and her friends were never tired of
expatiating on the beauty of the weather. She
had something to do every day, something that
took her away from the dry, dusty square. The
boys saw her drive off in the fresh morning, or
in the blaze of the meridian sun, her muslin frock
hidden by a dust-cloak that was all gauzy silk
and delicate lace. She looked like 'a fairy, Fluff
said, as he went yawning back to his favourite
corner, and stretched his weary limbs on the dusty
carpet beside a crowd of engines and coaches
that suggested Swindon or Crewe, and tried to
reproduce the last dreadful accident he had heard
his nurse and the housemaids talking about.

Poor Fluff was very weary of himself and of

life in general that wonderful summer. He hated
the square, he hated the streets, he hated Hyde
Park, he had ceased to care for his sheltie, for
he had nearly always a headache, and he told
Miss Perry that the pony's trot made his head
go "bumpity-bumpity-bump"—as if every tread
of those iron-shod hoofs were stamping upon his
brain. Every morning, with childish persistency,
he asked his mother to take him where she was
going; and every morning with the same light
musical laugh Mrs. Lerwick replied that it was
impossible.

"There will be only grown-up people there,
dearest. It's quite out of the question."

"Everything nice is always out of the question."

"Oh, Fluff, how ungrateful, when I took you
in the park yesterday evening, and you saw the
Princess, and I gave you an ice at Gunter's!"

"I hate the park—and the ice made me sick!"

"Then I'll never give you an ice again."

"Oh, that's bosh! It only made me sick
because I was sick before—I've had a sick headache all the summer."

"Fluff, how awfully you exaggerate. But I'll get Mr. Verriman to look at you."

"I don't want his looks. He looks at my tongue, and sighs; and he feels my pulse and sighs again; and he tries to look as if he were thinking; and then he sends me some beastly medicine—and then I'm no better."

There seemed a long interval of oppressive weather between Ascot week and Henley week, but at least Mother was nominally at home, though she was actually out nearly all day. Fluff was startled from a bad dream sometimes by the sound of the carriage stopping, and the shrill yap-yap of Spitz welcoming his mistress from ball or rout. She gave three parties in that interval—a dance; a musical evening, with opera singers and the finest instrumentalists in Europe; and a theatrical evening, with a little English one-act play, which had never been acted before, and which was so dull and trite that one might hope it would never be acted again, and a French Proverbe of that goody-goody order which the

Parisian actor reserves for the houses of the great, and the amusement of the English "mees."

Upon such festive evenings Paul and Fluff were allowed to stay up till after ten, in order to enjoy the privilege of standing at the top of the staircase, and seeing the earliest and least important guests "come grinning upstairs to jabber to Mother on the landing."

Eustace came from Elstree twice—on dental business—during that month of June. The dentist complained of him to poor little Miss Perry as a boy lost to all sense of honour, so seldom had he worn that silver regulating-plate which would have made him beautiful in the future, at the cost of considerable discomfort in the present.

"I can't play cricket with that beastly thing in my mouth," Eustace grumbled, and he gave the dentist to understand that good bowling was much more important than good teeth.

How Paul and Fluff envied this eldest brother, with his talk of cricket, at which he seemed to be a shining light—his chums, his tuck-woman— even his quarrels and fights! How much better the rough-and-tumble of school-life—mostly in the open air—than stagnation on a third floor in London, where the heat was hardly bearable between noontide and teatime. Eustace told them horrible stories of the cold-blooded cruelty of the masters, the fines, impositions, cutting off of holidays, but even those horrors didn't appal boys who were weary of home. He showed them one of his punishment tasks, at which Paul laughed the laugh of the scorner.

"Why, that's baby-work!" he cried. "I do three times as much Virgil with old Warren every morning. I'm reading the sixth book. Ain't it jolly? Better than the Arabian Nights!"

"You're a liar!" retorted Eustace, who hated books, and couldn't understand his brother liking them. "You know that's gammon."

Eustace went back to school directly the dentist had done with him. The silver plate had been through the fire, and had been re-adjusted. Eustace said it hurt his mouth worse than before; and it made him speak with the thickness

and indistinctness of an afflicted person. He
signalized his only appearance in the drawing-
room by taking a back fall on the parquet and
scratching that highly-polished surface with the
brads in his boots; and he left for Elstree de-
nounced by his mother as the clumsiest boy she
had ever met with; but as she gave him a hamper
from Fortnum's and a tip at parting he could not
think her unmotherly.

" Mother's a real good sort," he told his chums
at Elstree, "though she's a bit too much of a
swell."

July began in a manner to carry on the reputation of June. Farmers were complaining of
drought, newspapers were beginning to foreshadow
cholera, since the daily Press has long since made
up its mind that we are never to enjoy a glorious
summer without the dreaded guest from Asia.
Even in June, while the air is fresh, and summer
is young, that awful impalpable pilgrim is creeping across burning plains, and resting beside
poisoned wells, and faring steadily onward over
desert and city, towards the white-winged ships

in the harbour, to steal on board, unsuspected, a fatal stowaway.

There had been no "children's hour" since June began; for if Mrs. Lerwick happened to be at home at teatime there were always shrill chattering women in the morning room. Paul hated strange women, and was too proud to go in upon suffrance; but Fluff, who would go anywhere for cake, would creep in sometimes, and would be taken upon his mother's knee and kissed vehemently for half a minute, and then forgotten, while she talked to her friends over his golden head. He ate as many rich things as he liked on such occasions, rout cakes and bonbons, out of little silver wine-tasters. He was more bilious and headachy than usual, when he awoke on the morning after one of these tea-drinkings. His increasing languor made Miss Perry's feeble efforts at teaching more futile than ever, and words of one syllable seemed as difficult as if Fluff were a stranger to the English language.

And now it was July, and every one who loved the river was talking about Henley and Marlow.

Mr. and Mrs. Lerwick were going to see both regattas from a friend's house-boat—the *Paragon*, and verily a paragon of boats, for it was as big as an old-fashioned man-of-war, and decorated as elaborately as any fine lady's drawing-room.

Mrs. Lerwick mentioned the fact casually to her friends over Fluff's head, one afternoon, making light of the invitation, the boat, and the people, as became a fine lady.

"Mr. McCannister, the diamond man, has asked us, and we are going. It will be good fun. He is quite bearable—indeed, Tony rather likes him— but his daughters will want a great deal of snubbing if I am to enjoy myself."

"I shouldn't think you could stand them very long, though they say he has engaged Lord Leamington's *chef*," drawled a friend.

"Oh, we shall not be away more than four or five days—or a week, perhaps, if the river is too tempting. The McCannisters have a gondola, and a couple of real Venetians. Why, Fluff, what's the matter?" cried Mrs. Lerwick, discovering her youngest son in a flood of tears.

"You s-sa-said you wouldn't g-g-go away again till we all went to Heatherside," sobbed Fluff.

"Oh, you silly boy! This won't be going away —only for two or three days—just to see the regatta."

"Let me go wiv you."

"No, darling, I can't. It wouldn't be good for you."

"Why not?"

"Because—because—the river is so damp—and the wicked white fogs come up at night and swallow up little boys."

"No they don't. That's only baby-talk," said Fluff, swinging his legs in an ill-tempered way, and producing a very ugly lower lip. "Why can't I come?"

"Because it's Mr. McCannister's boat, darling. If it were father's boat I might take you— perhaps."

"You didn't take us to Windycum," sobbed Fluff, now become convulsive; whereupon bells were rung, and he was handed over to the servants; and the four shrill friends went away presently, kissing and cooing over Mrs. Lerwick to the last instant; and they dispersed their opinions among the multitude, to the effect that the odiousness of that youngest boy of the Lerwicks was only equalled by the brutal unmotherliness of his mother.

CHAPTER VI.

NOT ALL SUNSHINE,

THERE had never been such a glorious Henley week. The scientific people who look after the weather had to go back to the reign of William the Fourth for a summer that could parallel this summer which Paul and Fluff were spending wearily under the roasted slates in Palatine Square. All along the river bank at Henley the house-boats were ranged so closely that no one on the river could see the bank, and no one on the bank could see the river. And all the house-boats looked like gardens; till at night, when the many-coloured lanterns were lighted on deck, and the lamp light shone out of every window below, and they were all changed into fairy palaces. And Mrs. Lerwick had still so much of childish joy in her nature that she broke ever and anon into a little scream of rapture as she and her friends were borne smoothly along the dark water in Mr. McCannister's gondola. On every side the fairy palaces were shining, flags fluttering, rockets shooting skyward with a rushing sound, and then scattering in a shower of stars, ruby, emerald, sapphire. Fireworks were exploding, guitars tinkling, mandolines twanging, melodious voices singing on every side. Gounod's cradle-song mixed itself with Funicoli, funicola. Schubert's "Good-night" jarred against "Ta-ra-ra-boom-de-ay." But in this universal discord there was a kind of harmony; as if all dissonances were melted into concord by that broader, louder music of the rippling river and the summer wind.

Once in the midst of this gay scene Mrs. Lerwick, in a little burst of motherly feeling, exclaimed, "Oh, how I wish Fluff were here!"

But she reflected the next moment that it was nearly midnight, and that it was far better for her darling to be in bed and asleep.

The pity of it was that a boy might be in bed

and not asleep—and that Fluff had been sleeping very badly ever since the hot weather began. His mother was sitting on deck next day, under the gay striped awning, among the azaleas and orange trees, looking her prettiest in a creamy silk break-fast-gown, and comfortably conscious of her own prettiness. She was sitting in a little knot of superior people who could afford to look down upon their host, however well he "did them;" and the wit of the party had been "killing" in his remarks upon Mr. McCannister's frock-coat and sailor hat. Mrs. Lerwick gave herself no concern when the telegraph-boy appeared at the top of the steps with a bag full of telegrams, which a footman sorted and distributed.

Nobody is made uneasy by the sight of one of those buff envelopes nowadays; unless it is some over-anxious wife or mother ever apprehending evil news of her beloved.

"More invitations, I suppose," murmured Mrs. Lerwick, as the footman approached her with his salver.

There were three telegrams for her. Mr.

McCannister had received about twenty, and was lounging against one of the brass pillars that supported the awning, tearing open the envelopes.

There were three messages for Mrs. Lerwick. One from her dressmaker. Yes, the frock should be ready for the Duchess's ball. One from her jeweller, who deeply regretted that it was impossible to reset her opals in three days. The last was a longer message, signed "Julia Perry."

"I am sorry to trouble you while you are visiting, but Fritz is very ill. He was delirious all last night, and this morning Mr. Verriman seemed anxious. I asked if I should send for you, and he said yes. I hope I am not doing wrong."

Anthony Lerwick was at the other end of the boat, smoking, talking, laughing, in a little crowd of men, with one girl in their midst—a girl in a blue serge frock and a sailor hat, sitting on the brass rail—the kind of girl who always drifts in among the men, however many women there may be in a party, and as it were offers herself as a subject for chaff.

Mrs. Lerwick rushed to her husband, white as

her gown, trembling in every limb, the message held in her outstretched hand.

"What's the matter, Nell? Has that old har- ridan refused to make your frock?" asked Mr. Lerwick.

"Tony, I must go home instantly. Fluff is ill— delirious—dying."

She flung herself upon his shoulder, sobbing vehemently, while the blue serge girl dropped quietly off the brass rail, and slipped away to the ladies at the other end of the boat. The atmo- sphere had changed, and she had tact enough to know she wasn't wanted.

"Something amiss with the kid," she replied, when she was asked the meaning of Mrs. Lerwick's tragic movements. "I ain't on in that scene."

Lerwick took the telegram from his wife's hand and read it.

"Come, come, Nell, you needn't lose your head. When does the next London train start, Burton? Find out, like a good chap. There's nothing so much amiss—a little feverish and light-headed."

"I want to go home, home, directly," sobbed his

wife. "I wish I had never come here. We ought to have had our own house-boat, and the three boys with us. I hate myself for leaving them behind. Fluff so wanted to come! If there isn't a train directly, you'll get a special, won't you, Tony?"

There are moments and scenes in this life which burn themselves into even the shallowest mind. Feather-brained as Ellinor Lerwick was, she never forgot that morning at Henley—the sound of running water, the lights and shadows on the banks; the gathering crowd, alive with vivid colour; the perfume of the golden lilies in a tall, yellow vase beside her chair. All the beauty and charm of a riverside landscape under a July sky, all the movement and gaiety of a smartly-dressed crowd, were interwoven with the wild fear in her heart. "My darling, my idolized, neglected child is going to die."

Fluff lifted up his weary head, with a little cry of glad surprise, when his mother came into the room, and threw herself on her knees by his bed. He had just enough strength to put his poor dry sticks of arms round her neck. How they burnt with fever, those meagre little arms, from which the loose sleeves of his "jama" jacket fell away.

"My darling, my darling! Oh, how thin he has got—how thin! In two days."

"He has been getting thin for a long time, ma'am," said Nurse Pittman; "you may remember my mentioning it a month ago."

"Yes, yes; that was because he grew so fast. Darling, we will soon make you well."

The room was darkened, and wet kuskus blinds hung in front of the open window to cool the atmosphere. The noonday sun was beating fiercely on the slates above. It was a small low room, Fluff's "very own room," prettily furnished with white wood, and a little brass bedstead, and with roses and butterflies on the wall-paper. Everything was white and pink and gay-looking; but even that prettiness did not prevent the room feeling like an oven.

Mrs. Lerwick was too absorbed in Fluff to notice the atmosphere.

"What is Mr. Verriman doing for him?" she asked distractedly.

"He has a heffervescing draught every three hours, and he is to be kep' very quiet; and indeed, ma'am, you didn't ought to stay with him, you egzite him too much."

"Not stay with him, when I have come from Henley on purpose to nurse him! Let me read to you, my precious," sitting on the edge of the bed, and hugging the wasted little figure. "What shall it be? Grimm's Goblins or Hans Andersen?"

"I don't want to be read to; it only makes my head ache more and more," moaned Fluff.

"Not if I read very softly, dearest."

"You can't read softly. Only Auntie can read not to hurt one when one's ill. Miss Perry has been reading to me—awfully badly, but not so bad as you."

"Oh, Fluff, how unkind of you," remonstrated his mother, beginning to cry.

"Don't, don't, mummy; I didn't mean to be rude. If you cry like that," Mrs. Lerwick growing hysterical, "you'll make me delirious again. I was delirious all night, and I dreamt of such awful things—big heads without bodies—heads that came hopping into the room—and one was Bluebeard, with his throat cut like the footman who cut his throat in George Street."

"Who told you that? I suppose it was you, Nurse. It is shameful that a child should be told such things."

"I never told him nothing of the sort, ma'am. And if I did it wouldn't have done him any more harm than the pantomime last Christmas. He talked more about Bluebeard than he did about the footman," retorted Nurse Pittman, who had forty pounds a year to her wages, and rarely condescended to undertake anything but "a lady's first baby," as per advertisement. She was an old-fashioned nurse, who set up the light of nature and long experience against modern training, and was not at all the kind of person to accept reproof meekly.

Mrs. Lerwick stopped in the room for some hours, moaning over Fluff at intervals, and worrying him from time to time with offers of things he did not want—a grape, a little lemonade, some more Eau-de-Cologne to dab his burning forehead. Life was all pain and weariness to the poor, little, feverish child; and these ministrations of his mother's were the last straws. And yet he loved her well enough to be glad that she had come back to him, and to kiss her every now and then with his parched lips.

There were several interruptions to the quiet of the sick room during those hours of maternal watching. Servants came with messages. Could Mrs. Lerwick see the housekeeper for a few minutes? Or could she see the forewoman from Mrs. Black, the florist, who had called about the decorations for the dinner-party next week? These messengers were snubbed and sent away; but later in the afternoon there came a messenger who would not be denied. This was Babette, who announced that a young person from Madame Violette was in Madame's room, waiting to try on her ball-gown for the *fête* of Madame la Duchesse.

Mrs. Lerwick gave a little sigh as she rose to

obey this summons.   If Fluff should be worse that
ball finery would be sadder than sackcloth.   But
no, he was going to get better.   She counted the
days on her fingers.   Saturday, Sunday, Monday,
Tuesday.   Children pick up so quickly.   No
doubt he would be well by Wednesday; and she
was frightening herself uselessly.   She stooped to
kiss him, and hurried after Babette.

Paul, who was moping over a book in the schoolroom, ran out into the corridor, and threw his arms
about his mother.

" Is he very bad, mother ? "

" No, dear, not bad, only very feverish."

" It's this beastly house, exclaimed Paul, vin-
dictively ; " I hate the London season."

"When he's better I'll pack you all off to
Heatherside."

" Alone ? "

" You'll have Miss Perry and Miss Warren."

Paul whistled contemptuously.

"A precious pair ! But it will be better to be
with them at Heatherside than in this gloomy
hole."

"Oh, Paul! think of all the little boys who would love to live in Palatine Square."

"I can't think of 'em. I don't believe there are any such boys. I'd rather live among the bird-shops in Seven Dials. There's some life there."

Mrs. Lerwick offered him a kiss, her universal panacea, and hurried away to the mademoiselle from Madame Violette, a rather airified made-moiselle, who scarcely condescended to speak to the client while she tried on the ball-gown, but turned Mrs. Lerwick about as if she had been a lay figure, and pinned her and pinched her, and slashed the satin upon her shoulders with a pair of cold scissors in a most alarming way.

Mrs. Lerwick, contemplating those ivory shoul-ders in the cheval-glass, against a raw edge of pale pink satin, asked in rather stumbling French whether the bodice was not somewhat too *décolleté*, whereupon the ma'amselle shrugged her own lean shoulders and replied severely in English—

"Dat is 'ow de bodice carry himself zis season, madame," and would condescend to no further discussion.

H

She folded the gown, assisted respectfully by Babette, and a footman was rung for to carry Ma'amselle's basket downstairs, and when she was gone Mrs. Lerwick sat down in her blue satin bergère and cried herself to sleep, exhausted by the joyousness of last night on the river, and by the sorrowfulness of to-day. She slept till the clash of china and silver in the next room told her that the tea-table was made ready, and her dreams were a jumble of coloured lanterns and star-showering rockets, sick boys, and racing eights.

CHAPTER VII.

WHAT THE DOCTOR SAID.

ANTHONY LERWICK was not the kind of man to hang about his son's sick room, being essentially an out-of-door person, but he did the next best thing, which was to see the doctor who was attending Fluff, and, after briefest conference with him, to drive to Cavendish Square, and make an appointment with the physician in whose power of diagnosis the great world at that time believed. Though London bristles with clever doctors, there is always one consulting physician whom every one talks about as if he were Æsculapius in a frock-coat. Now Sir Joseph Jerman was *the* man this season, and every ailing creature in Mayfair believed in his power of healing.

He was a very busy man, therefore, and it was only the father's evident anxiety that induced him to make an appointment for that evening. He promised to cut short his own dinner-hour in order to see the little boy in Palatine Square at nine o'clock. He could not possibly see him earlier. And so it was arranged that Mr. Verriman and the physician should meet in Fluff's bedroom while fashionable London was dining; and this was the most cheering news that Mr. Lerwick could take home to his wife.

She kissed him and praised him for his thoughtfulness, and at nine o'clock she was sitting at Fluff's bedside waiting for the doctors. She had to leave before anything was done. Mothers and all such rubbish had to be cleared away to give the great man a free hand. He asked the little boy's nurse two or three questions, and then dismissed her with a look which indicated an absolute contempt for that highly respectable person.

Mr. and Mrs. Lerwick had only a quarter of an hour to wait; but it was one of those long quarter-hours which people remember for all their lives to come ; an interval of agonizing fear which can be recalled distinctly many years afterwards, with all the sensations of the actual moment.

"Oh, doctor, is he dreadfully ill ? " Mrs. Lerwick asked, holding out her clasped hands imploringly, as the grey-headed great man came into the room. "Is it typhoid, or typhus, or anything incurable ? "

"There is absolutely nothing the matter with your son, madam. You have only been killing him."

"Killing him! Oh, Sir Joseph, what can you mean ? "

"Every principle of hygiene has been violated. In the hottest summer we have had in England for thirty years, you keep that frail, sensitive child in a room the cubical contents of which would be inadequate for a garret in a cottage."

Cubical contents! Mrs. Lerwick looked despairingly at her husband, and her tremulous lips whispered involuntarily, "What are cubical contents ? "

"You allow gas to be burnt in his room all night."

"What other light should we have ? Gas is so safe for children's rooms."

"Safe! Yes, safe to burn up their lungs. I don't want to say anything unkind, Mrs. Lerwick ; but it is sad to see a beautifully-made child—with nothing organically wrong about him—wasting away as your child is wasting away—just perishing of improper treatment—badly housed, improperly fed, kept without sufficient air or exercise, stifled under a miserable low ceiling, baked to death in an ill-ventilated oven of a room. It is saddening that such ignorance should exist—in Palatine Square—after all the books that have been written and the lectures that have been given on domestic sanitation."

Sir Joseph Jerman paced the small schoolroom to and fro like a lion in a cage—like a fine old grey-headed lion. The folly and ignorance of the rich were always more irritating to him than the mistakes of the poor. He expected the poor to be ignorant, and he bore with them, and taught them, and was tender with them; but he was indignant with the pretty young mothers who thought more of their frocks than of their children.

"What are we to do, Sir Joseph?" Mrs. Lerwick asked helplessly.

"Mr. Verriman knows what to do. There is very little to be done; but there is a great deal to be undone. To begin with, the boy must be removed to a larger room."

"But every bedroom is occupied. This is such a small house as to bedrooms."

"Nonsense, Nell," muttered her husband, quickly. "He can have your morning room."

"Yes, we might put a bed in my morning room, only——"

She was going to say that it would be very inconvenient in the height of the season; but something in the doctor's face checked her.

"Your morning room by all means, if it is airy and cheerful."

"Oh, it is quite the cheerfulest room in the house."

"Move him into it this evening. No gas, re-member."

"Oh, I have no gas in my morning room. It is so destructive to curtains and ornaments."

"And to human life also, strange to say," said the doctor, grimly. "As soon as he is able for the journey you will send him to the seaside."

"He can go to our own place."

"Where is that?"

"In Dorsetshire, near Bournemouth."

"A charming place no doubt, but he will require a more bracing air—Margate, for instance."

"Oh, Sir Joseph, such a horrid Cockney place!"

"He will go there for the air. The Cockneys needn't get in his way. I'll come and see him again next week, and talk the business over with you."

Sir Joseph had shaken hands with Mr. and Mrs. Lerwick, and had gone a little way downstairs with Mr. Verriman, when the lady ran after him.

"Oh, doctor, please don't think me frivolous, but there is to be a very smart ball next Wednesday, and I should love to go to it, if my darling were well enough by that time."

"I'll come and see him on Wednesday after-noon. If my instructions are obeyed I dare say he'll be well enough for you—to leave him."

Fluff was visibly better within three days of his removal to the large airy room, and under those strict rules of dietary laid down by Sir Joseph Jerman. Mrs. Lerwick was not allowed to see much of him during these three days, as one of Sir Joseph's injunctions had been extreme quiet.

"You had better get a trained nurse—a young woman," he told Verriman. "I don't like that bustling nurse in the black silk gown. The governess seems a good little creature. She has a quiet manner and a mild eye. Keep the bustling woman away from him, and the mother. He'll do well enough if he gets a fair chance."

The physician had no reason to complain when he came on Wednesday. The boy was sitting up in one of his mother's prettiest chairs, with Pincher for his play-fellow—Pincher, who stuck his claws into the delicate lace frillings of pillows and chair backs, and who scratched for rats in the corners of satin sofas. Fluff had made himself thoroughly at home in the morning room.

"Mother's coming to tea with me, if I'm well enough to-morrow afternoon," he told his physician. "Won't that be fun, mother coming to tea as my visitor in her own room!"

"Capital! And would you like to go to the seaside next week?"

"Wouldn't I, just!"

"And whom would you like to have with you?"

Fluff's countenance fell.

"Mother said it would be the two governesses, Paul's and mine," he said. "They won't be much fun. Miss Warren hates dogs, and Miss Perry can't run. She ain't a bit of good at games. I know the person I should like," added Fluff.

"Who is that?"

"The little Auntie."

"A sister of yours, Mrs. Lerwick?" asked the doctor.

"Yes, my youngest sister."

" She would hardly be equal to the responsibility of looking after your little invalid, perhaps," hazarded Sir Joseph, " if she is much younger than you."

" She is eight years younger ; but she is a very old-maidish, prim little person, and doesn't a bit mind responsibility."

" Then might it not be wise to let this young lady accompany your children to Margate or Ramsgate, if she could be spared ? "

" Oh, I dare say she might be spared, and I know she would like to come.   She would do anything for the children.   She adores my children. She often comes to stay with us when we are at Heatherside ; and she sees a great deal of the children, and knows all about their ways almost better than I know them myself."

" That is quite possible," assented Sir Joseph, with grave politeness.

Fluff went dancing about the room on shaky legs, crying—

" The little Auntie—the little Auntie ! Hip, hip, hurrah ! for the little Auntie."

He ran to the door and opened it, and screamed up the staircase, in his shrillest voice —

"Paul, Paul, Paul! we're going to Margate with the little Auntie! No Warren, no Perry—only the little Auntie!"

"Not Margate!" exclaimed Mrs. Lerwick, in an imploring voice. "Anything but Margate. How could I tell people my children had gone to Margate?"

"This little man won't want to see me any more," said Sir Joseph, stooping down to kiss Fluff's fair forehead. "He will do very well now, Mrs. Lerwick, if you take a lesson from what has happened, and obey all Mr. Verriman's instructions."

Paul cannoned against the doctor as he ran into the room.

"Are we going to Margate instead of Heatherside?" he exclaimed. "How jolly!"

There is an innate vulgarity in children only to be eradicated by early association with smart people.

CHAPTER VIII.

THE CHILDREN'S PLAYFELLOW.

THE little Auntie had only to be told that one of her nephews was ailing, and that her society might be of some service to him. There was no paid attendant, tempted by the promise of high wages, who would have answered Mrs. Lerwick's summons more promptly than it was answered by Miss Dorothea Hampden. No entreaties were needed to bring this lady to Palatine Square. She had no sense of ill-usage at not having been invited to share in the glories of the London season. She needed but to be told that Fritz had been almost dangerously ill, and that she was the most eligible person to take him and his brother to the seaside.

"You will have Perry and Pittman, and I shall

send a groom to look after pony-carriages and things ; so there will be no drudgery," wrote her sister.

Dora smiled at this passage about drudgery. As if there were any labour that would have seemed common or unclean to her, if it were to be done for those dear children. Often and often in her day-dreams she had pictured to herself what her life might have been like had her sister's husband been a struggling professional man, instead of a millionaire; how she might have taken care of the boys in a country cottage, and taught them, and sewed and washed and ironed for them ; and how her days, instead of being just a little aimless and monotonous, as they were now, would have been full of delightful work and duty.

Dorothea was only twenty-four, but as all her people and most of her friends and acquaintances had made up their minds that she was not likely to marry, she had, with one reservation, accepted their view of her case, and had resigned herself to the possibility of life-long spinsterhood. For if that one person whose image occupied so large a place in the quiet depths of her mind were to forget her in the far-off land whither he had gone, she knew there was no one else in the world who would ever win her liking. She was one of those quiet little people whose thoughts lie deep in a shy silence, and who know not what it is to change.

She was the youngest of four sisters, of whom three were married; two of them well, one of them rather badly, since a country Vicar with a large parish and a small income was considered a very poor match for the sister of Ellinor Hampden, who had married millions.

Georgiana, who had married only three years since, was now giving the tone to society in an Indian province, as the wife of a highly-placed official.

These three ladies had all been accounted handsome; and their sister, Dorothea, as the youngest and least attractive of the brood, had long ago been given a kind of Cinderella place in the family circle. She was not asked to sit in the chimney-corner, or to clean pots and pans; but

she was allowed, and even expected, to run up
and down stairs and fetch gloves, parasols, books,
and pocket-handkerchiefs, for the other three, who
were encouraged in careless habits by the handi-
ness of a willing little sister.

That was Dorothea's chief characteristic. She
was always the Little Sister. She was not a
creature of abnormal smallness like Little Dorrit.
No one could have mistaken her for a child when
she was a grown-up woman. But she was small
and slender, very delicately fashioned, with a foot
arched like an Arab chief's, and a tapering hand,
and a waist that made everybody else's waist seem
thick and clumsy. If she had been very beautiful,
people would have called her Titania; but as she
was popularly supposed to be rather plain, in
comparison with the three tall sisters with their
vivid Devonshire complexions and bright hair,
she was commonly described as insignificant. Yet
plainness, actual plainness, could hardly exist
with large dark-grey eyes, and a very expressive
mouth, and a broad intelligent forehead. There
were, indeed, no positive faults in Dora's face, for

even her nose, though belonging to no established order, was neither pug nor snub, and her complexion, though wanting in colour, was clear as fine ivory. In a plainer family she might have taken rank as a pretty little girl; but the three beautiful sisters overshadowed her, and had always taken care, in the most good-natured way, to let her know her place.

Mr. Eustace Hampden, of Mill Park, near Bideford, was a Devonshire squire in a very small way. The Devonshire Hampdens had migrated from Oxfordshire after the Civil Wars, and claimed to be lineal descendants from the famous tribune who got his death-wound on Chalgrove Field. They had owned broader acres in the past than that diminished estate which belonged to Dora's father; but this gentleman, having no sons, and having been lucky in marrying his daughters in the bloom of their young beauty, found his income sufficient for himself and his only remaining girl—more especially as Dora had no troublesome desire for expensive gaieties, had never suggested a season in town, and was able to enjoy herself summer after summer at a regulation round of garden-parties, and to dance at any ball which local hospitality, or local subscription, might provide for rural youth and beauty.

This was the young woman who came flying up to Palatine Square as fast as a South-Western Express could bring her, and who sat in Mother's morning room with Fluff on her lap, and Paul sitting on the arm of her chair, both of them hugging her with all their might, while Pincher clambered over the group and licked all three faces indiscriminately.

"Stacie is coming home to-morrow, and we're all going off to Ramsgate next week," said Paul. "Ain't that prime? Though I wouldn't mind even stopping here, now we've got some one to play with us."

"And to love us," said Fluff, between two kisses.

"Oh, Fluff, as if Mother didn't love you," remonstrated Dora.

"Of course Mother loves me—when she has time. Mummy loves me dearly once or twice a week—but you love me always."

"Mother was the prettiest woman at the Duchess's ball," said Paul. "I heard her tell father so."

"How did she know?" asked Fluff. "One doesn't know how pretty one is one's own self, does one? I don't."

"She heard the Prince tell the Duchess," explained Paul.

"Isn't his nose beautifully cool?" Fluff asked about Pincher, after a particularly energetic lick.

"I think his manners are particularly cool," answered the little Auntie.

"Ah! it wouldn't do with some of Mother's friends," said Paul. "He'd get poisoned with the stuff they put on their faces."

"Oh, Paul, how can you know anything about it?"

"So," answered Paul, pointing with his forefinger to his eyes. "That's how."

"And so, my dear Stacie is coming here to-morrow," said Aunt Dora, quite resigned to be pushed almost out of her chair by Pincher, who had established himself behind her back, and who didn't like to be crowded. "Is he as handsome as ever?"

"I don't know anything about handsomeness. He's just the same as he always was, only a little bigger and a little thicker. *He* gets air and exercise, so he grows. We stop where we are."

"But you have had your ponies all the summer."

"Who cares for ponies in summer? They had better have had their shoes off, and been saving up for the hunting next November," said Paul. "What I want in summer is cricket, or rowing. I ought to have been at Elstree, instead of being kept at home to keep a baby like Fluff company."

"*I* don't want you!" cried Fluff, indignantly. "You're always as cross as two sticks; and you're no company for me."

"Ah, but Mother thinks you'd fret if you were alone."

"Well, now you are going to have lots of air and exercise; and cricket too, perhaps; and golf, and tennis," said the little Auntie, "and we shall have no end of fun."

"Have you ever been at Ramsgate?"

"Only for a few hours at a time, when my cousin Jack was curate at Sandwich, and I went on a visit to him and his wife."

"Sandwich! What a funny name for a place! Mother says Ramsgate is awfully vulgar; but not quite so objectionable as Margate."

Miss Warren, who could be trusted to do anything requiring firmness of hand and business capacity, had obliged Mrs. Lerwick by going down to Ramsgate for the day, and interviewing agents, and looking at houses. In this quest she perambulated the whole length of the east and west cliffs, and investigated innumerable houses in her rapid and decisive manner, forming her opinion on the first room into which she was ushered, and wasting no time upon inspecting unwholesome upper floors after detecting dust in the dining-room. Finally she decided upon a fine house in Imperial Crescent, considered quite the most aristocratic quarter of the popular watering-place.

Thither on the following Monday were to journey a couple of maids and a footman, with

Miss Perry to look after them; and on Tuesday the three boys and their Aunt were to travel, with only Pittman in attendance.

"You'll have four evenings with us," said Mrs. Lerwick to her sister. "I really must take you about a little"—condescendingly—"to the opera, and to some of my parties."

"Not to your parties, Nell; I have nothing smart enough for them."

"You don't mean to say that you have come without an evening frock!" exclaimed Mrs. Lerwick, almost as horrified as if she had supposed that her sister travelled without a tooth-brush.

"Oh no, I have two evening frocks in my trunk. One of them would do very well for the opera; and I should think it so sweet of you to take me."

"I'll take you to-night. It's *Tannhaüser*. Of course you adore Wagner?"

"I mean to worship him when I hear more of him. I've heard so little modern music. Why, Fluff, what's the matter? Has Pincher bitten you?"

Fluff had suddenly melted—or rather exploded —into tears—indignant tears.

"What's the good of your coming to be with us if you're going to the opera with her?" he asked, angrily. "You'll be no more good to us than *she* is"—pointing at his mother.

"Fluff, Fluff, that isn't nice of you. It's quite right of your mother to go to the opera—all grown-up people like to go—and it can't hurt you for me to go. You will be asleep before the opera begins."

"No I shan't—I don't go to sleep easily. I want you to read to me after I'm in bed."

"The doctor said there was to be no reading after you was in bed, Master Frederick," said Pittman, who had just appeared upon the scene— heading a contingent of flunkey and maid bearing materials for tea — table — kettle — tea-tray—but not carrying so much as a plate of bread-and-butter herself. "You was to have the room kep' quiet and just go to sleep."

"The doctor's an ass. Everybody's an ass," cried Fluff, furious at this interference.

His aunt talked to him seriously in her gentle little way—and made him understand the selfishness of his desire to keep her in the house all the evening when she could be of no use to him. She would have willingly given up that great delight of hearing a famous opera, if her self-sacrifice could have done her darling any good; but she knew that it was for Fluff's best good to grapple at once with the demon of selfishness. She had been with the family at Heatherside long enough to know how that familiar demon had been encouraged and developed in poor little Fluff by his mother's treatment of him, which was blind indulgence, tempered by intervals of neglect.

"I shall stop with you till your bedtime, dear," she concluded cheerily, after her mild remonstrance.

"Oh no, you won't. You'll be going down to dinner."

"Not till eight, Master Frederick, and you ought to be abed before eight," said Nurse.

"I wish you'd mind your own business, and not chip in when you ain't asked," to the nurse, and then fretfully to Dora. "You'll be all the rest of the time dressing."

"Dearest, it's only half-past five. Do you think I take two hours and a half to dress?"

"Mother does. At least, she takes a jolly long time."

"I'll dress directly after tea, and I promise not to be away more than half an hour."

"And then we'll play spillikens."

"Anything you like."

Aunt Dora kept her word, and came back to Fluff's room by-and-by in a pretty pink frock, which gave just the right touch of warm colour to the pale clearness of her complexion.

Fluff and Paul were sprawling on the Persian rug in front of the open window, beginning to be very tired of each other, and of the summer evening, and longing for Ramsgate.

"Mother says the place will swarm with niggers at this time of the year," said Paul.

"Real negroes like them as Miss Warren read about in Stanley's book?"

"You mustn't say them as—it isn't English."

"Ain't it ? It's my language, and it will do for me," Fluff replied haughtily. "Will they be real black persons, or only Christy minstrels ? "

"Christys, of course. The real ones wouldn't be any fun. Auntie"—as Dora appeared, and they both sprang up to receive her—"that's a very jolly frock ; and now come and sit on the floor and play spillikens."

"Not on the floor, Fluff, in my party frock."

"Ah, you're just as bad as Mother ; you think of your frock first and of us afterwards. You said you hadn't got a party frock."

"Not good enough for a Duchess's party."

"Oh, the Duchess ain't much to look at. She came here to dinner, and Mother made no end of a fuss about it. I saw her from the top of the staircase. She looked like a haycock tied up in pink satin. Besides, she has given her evening party. That's all over. She won't ask Mother twice in a season."

"Oh, but London parties in general are too smart for me."

"That's why Mother doesn't have you here in

the season," said Fluff. "I heard her tell one of her friends that you were very nice and dear, but not pretty enough to get on in society."

"What rot!" exclaimed Paul, who had some vague glimmering of the courtesy due to women younger than Miss Warren. "Auntie's quite pretty enough. Nobody wants pretty people all over the shop."

"Oh, we like her as she is," assented Fluff, patronizingly. "We don't care about your not being pretty, you know."

"I hope not, darling. You love me for my own sake."

"And because you'll play any game we want, and don't go to parties every night like Mother does. I'm very glad you're not pretty," concluded Fluff, decisively. "Pretty people ought never to have any children."

"But then everybody would grow up ugly," objected Paul, taking a broader view of the question.

"It would be a world of monsters," said Dora, laughing.

"Who cares? Pretty people who go to three parties a night can't want children—or dogs. I wouldn't mind Mother neglecting *us* if she hadn't let Spitz get canker in his ears ever so bad before she sent him to Jewell to be cured."

Aunt Dora changed the conversation. She would never listen to unfilial criticism; but it was very difficult to keep that fiery little member, Fluff's tongue, within proper limits.

Stacie came home on Tuesday morning, brown and tall, and healthy-looking, a startling contrast to his younger brothers. He had grown out of his clothes in a single term; and Mrs. Lerwick sent for the tailor before he had been in Palatine Square half an hour.

"You are absolutely disreputable," she exclaimed. "I think you must stretch yourself out somehow at your everlasting cricket. It can't be actual growth. Why, you are nearly as tall as I am."

She stood beside her eldest son in front of the cheval-glass. How tall he looked! And what a rough brown creature, with freckled cheeks and a sunburnt nose! At this rate he would be a young man in three or four years; and she would find herself going about the world with a grown-up son. And she had thought of herself up to this moment as a girl—a married girl. She had chosen all girlish things for her attire, and had rejected everything ungirlish as too old—heavy colours—brocades—velvets—gold embroideries—she had disdained all these splendours as unsuitable; and now in a few years—with a grown-up son—she must bid good-bye to girlishness.

Well, he was not a daughter. There was comfort at least in that. She would not be called a chaperon. She would not have to sit on a bench and receive sour looks from an indignant young woman suffering under a dearth of partners. Eustace would be able to find partners for himself —and she might go on waltzing without qualms of conscience.

CHAPTER IX.

A SUMMER ISLAND.

Ah! what a life that was in Imperial Crescent.
What a glorious interval of utter idleness! There
were to be no lessons for Paul, for Miss Warren
was off duty, and had taken a holiday engagement
with a very magnificent family in Scotland; and,
although the gentle Perry was with them, Fluff
claimed immunity from even words of three letters,
in his character of convalescent. What a change
from the dull and dusty streets to sun-baked cliffs
and far-stretching corn-fields! Instead of the
smoke-blackened tree-tops of a London square,
the children's morning eyes looked out over one
of the prettiest bays in England—that crescent
of sea between Ramsgate and Deal. And before
them stretched those broad downs that every

Englishman loves. They were looking over the great waterway of the nations. Over the azure and emerald of that summer sea they saw the great ships going out to the East; the gaily-painted pleasure steamers plying backwards and forwards, crammed with humanity; the little sailing-boats skimming about, looking no bigger or more substantial than children's toys. And opposite, in the bright, clear mornings or in the golden afternoons, they sometimes saw the white cliffs of France.

"I thought *we* had the only white cliffs," said Paul. "I'm sure we make as much fuss about 'em as if no other country had any."

If the daylight was lovely on that happy shore, the night was no less beautiful, for first there were the Thanet stars, planets, and constellations, which were so superior to the stars in London that Fluff would hardly believe they were the same.

"They're like them, only better," he said; whereupon Paul entered upon a disquisition on astronomy which made the rest of the party, including his aunt and elder brother, think very poorly of themselves.

"How that old woman does make you sap," Eustace exclaimed contemptuously. "I'm afraid they'll think you an awful smug at the 'Varsity."

Miss Warren had crammed her pupil with that solid and useful information which is apt, in this frivolous age, to make the possessor obnoxious to his friends and acquaintances. Paul was always bringing out learned coin from his intellectual treasury; coin which was received by Eustace with derision, and by Aunt Dora with a warmth of interest and desire for instruction which anybody could see was pure acting.

"You know you're boring Auntie with that long preach about the cliffs," Eustace remonstrated, when his brother had been expatiating upon some of the wonders of geology, with all the newest views derived from Geikie. "What does she care whether they're argillaceous or confusedly crystalline, as long as we don't tumble over them? If she wants to know anything about jolligy she can read it in a book—better than you can tell her."

"Oh, but I like to hear him, I do, indeed, Stacie."

"Well, I don't. And he'd better shut up, unless he wants his head punched," grumbled Eustace; and Paul remembered with a sardonic smile that Galileo was bullied, and Giordano Bruno burnt alive.

Paul thought he would hardly mind being burnt alive if he were sure that posterity would put up statues to him and make a shrine of his birthplace hundreds of years afterwards. He was a prig, and he was conceited, but he was the kind of unpleasant boy who is sometimes the father of the distinguished man. Eustace was frankly—nay, even boastfully—ignorant. He was assured that he would never have to work for his living, and that a fine bowler has the world at his feet. His own ambition was a cavalry regiment; but his mother had made up her mind that she would not have any of her sons shot, so he had to reconcile himself to the idea of being only a cricketer; and he saw before him a roving career all over England, bowling out adversaries from every county—and even from the remotest English-speaking colony. It was as a bowler that his laurels had been won.

K

He had had his name in the *Sportsman* after the Elstree-Cheam match.

Paul meant to go into Parliament, and to startle the House nightly by knowing everything that nobody else knew. He had put the younger Pitt before himself as a model, and sometimes dropped from drowsiness into dreamland, muttering, " A heaven-born minister," or " How I leave—love— leave—my country ! "

Miss Warren had impressed upon him that he must be and do something. Nature and fortune had done much for him. Labour and perseverance must do the rest. He didn't like Miss Warren ; but he understood dimly that she was useful to him, and that even Elstree might be a retrograde step in his intellectual journey. After Elstree would come Harrow—where he would get scholar- ships—but perhaps pass them on to poorer boys— and then Oxford—Balliol or Magdalen—one of the reading men's colleges—not Christchurch.

Fluff wished to be a middy or a "gentleman jock." He had not quite decided which.

" If I keep racehorses, I'll take good care they

shall win, for I'll ride 'em myself," said Fluff, who had made up his mind that there was something rotten in his father's training-stable.

He might have heard the footmen talking—or he may have had Delphic hints from Tandy, who was too good a servant to say right out that his master, in the matter of horseflesh, was a fool.

Tandy was with them at Ramsgate. That fact filled Fluff's cup of gladness with just the last drop of nectar. Paul was almost as glad; though he would not for worlds have admitted that Tandy's presence could make any difference to him. They rode their shelties every morning before breakfast, after just a cup of milk and a slice of bread-and-butter, which Auntie called their " chota hazri."

" What's 'chota hazri'?" Fluff asked, the first time he heard the phrase.

" It's an Indian expression."

" I know ; it's that horrid hot pickle which looks as if it was nice, and burns the roof of one's mouth," said Paul.

"No, Paul, for once you're wrong. 'Chota hazri' is Hindustani for a small breakfast."

"How should I know Hindustani? I can't think how you come to be so learned about Indian words," said Paul, who thought himself insulted.

It was a small thing, surely, to make Aunt Dora turn as red as a rose, but the rose tint was there, and Paul became disagreeably curious.

"Where did you learn Hindustani, Auntie? You've never been in India."

"And I never learnt Hindustani, Paul; but when your Aunt Georgie was engaged, and when Sir Henry Mandeville was a great deal with us, and his sister, and a cousin of his in the same service—— "

"Oh, Auntie, how red you are!" cried Fluff.

They were sitting at a cosy round table, taking their second breakfast, after a long ride in a world that seemed enchanted, so thrilling was the freshness of the air, and the sparkle of the dew, and the unspeakable splendour of colouring over sea and sky; a little way inland, past hop-gardens, where the young green of the blossom showed pale against the dark green of the foliage; past fields of Indian maize with broad flapping leaves; and then back to the coast, past broad plains of bearded barley, and above that lovely bay, where the shallow sea looks a lake. Aunt Dora had been walking with Pincher and a book, up and down the promenade, or on the lawn which belonged exclusively to those superior persons who lived in Imperial Crescent; but wherever Pincher was, the book came off second best, for he was a dog who required continual attention, and couldn't amuse himself for five minutes without sympathy and assistance. He wanted his ball thrown for him, or somebody's gown to hang on to with his adamantine jaws. All Aunt Dora's flounces showed the marks of Pincher's resolute little teeth.

"You must never tell a lady she's blushing," Stacie said gravely; "it's beastly bad form."

"And you must never say 'beastly,'" retorted Fluff. "Mother says it's a low, common word."

"I've heard her say it herself, though, when her dressmaker disappointed her," said Stacie.

Dora's flaming cheeks had lost a little of their colour during this brief skirmish, and she hoped the question had dropped. It might not have been renewed, perhaps, had she been self-possessed enough to start some fresh topic; but she wasn't, and Paul returned to the charge with a deadly persistence.

"Did Sir Henry teach you Hindustani words?" he asked.

"No; Sir Henry was too much occupied with Aunt Georgie."

"Was it his sister taught you, or his cousin?"

"Nobody taught me. I just heard Hindustani words spoken, mixed up with English, anyhow, and I picked them up—a very few words."

"Was Sir Henry's cousin a man or a woman?" asked Paul.

"A man," answered Dora, the colour coming back in a wave of fire.

"Did you like him?"

"Oh, I liked him well enough."

"And did he like you?"

"How should I know?"

" Is he a soldier ? "

" No ; a civilian."

" What a poor creature a man must be to put up with being a civilian if he could have been a soldier," said Eustace, to whose mind the name of the civil service sounded contemptible.

A regiment—a mere line regiment even—had a noble sound. The Midlandshire, the Northshire, the Southshire, the Anyshire. It conjured up the roll of drums, the blare of trumpets, the scaling ladder, the mounted breach, the enemy's broken lines, the Victoria Cross. But a civilian—a man who sat at a desk and wrote letters, or even worse, kept accounts. How could anybody be interested in such a person? Eustace wanted to hear no more about him.

Fluff was not so easily satisfied. He hated book learning; but was keenly curious about people. He had acquired a very grown-up vocabulary from his conversation with servants, and frequent listening to gossip not intended for his ears, and with the vocabulary a large stock of very grown-up thoughts, which jarred upon grown-up hearers when they dropped from those rosy lips.

Fluff, who had been engaged with a basin of porridge and treacle, now came—like a giant refreshed—to the attack.

"He wasn't in love with you, was he, Auntie?"

"Of course not, Fluff. What an absurd question."

"No, it ain't absurd. It ain't absurd to be in love. All our housemaids are in love. I've heard them talk about their young men. Sarah has a young man in Palatine Square; and she walks out with the postman in Dorsetshire. She says it doesn't matter her having two, because neither of them will ever know anything about the other."

"I'm very sorry you should listen to such vulgar talk."

"I don't listen, Auntie. I only hear when I can't help hearing. They *will* talk with the door open, when they're cleaning the rooms, and I'm playing in the schoolroom, and I hear them."

"You should call out, and let them know you're there."

"Oh, I don't see why I should spoil the fun like that."

"How can you be curious about people who don't belong to you?"

"Because they are people," replied Fluff, like an infant philosopher, "and I want to know all about them."

This time the conversation seemed to have drifted comfortably away from the subject which had hung so vivid a flag on Dorothea's cheeks. The little Auntie had quite recovered her usual happy calmness, presently, when Pincher took them all out on the "Prom." It was generally Pincher who took them out of doors, for he so evidently expected it of them every time they rose from a meal—or even from a chair—that his vivacity led to a frequent running out on to the lawn, and thence to the Promenade, or "Prom," as the boys always called it.

Dorothea was sitting at the end of the "Prom" half an hour afterwards, when she found to her

cost that she was not yet out of the wood.
Children seldom forget any topic which has
awakened their curiosity.

"I've come to sit by you and rest," said Fluff,
sidling up to her, while his brothers played tennis
with a highly respectable family in the sacred
enclosure, whose acquaintance they had been
allowed to make. " It's such spoony work playing
pat-ball with girls. Stacie wouldn't do it if he
wasn't mashed on that carroty Miss Thomson."

"Fluff, you mustn't use such vulgar words.
'Mashed!' 'Carroty!' I'm positively ashamed
of you."

"Well, I don't know how I am to talk if I can't
use the same words as other boys. Auntie, why
did you never marry anybody?"

"What a startling question, Fluff."

" No, but why? "

" Perhaps I was never asked."

" Is that why you're so fond of us? "

"Perhaps."

"Well, I'm very glad nobody ever cared for
you ; though I think it's very queer of people not

to like you. But it would have been horrid for you to marry."

" Why horrid, dear ? "

" Because if you were married you wouldn't be our little Auntie any more."

" Dearest, I should not be the least little bit less your Auntie, or the least bit less fond of you."

" Oh yes you would. *He* would always be wanting you. He would call us 'those tiresome boys,' and send us out of the room. He would blow you up if you had us at your house too often. He would be afraid we should meddle with his guns. He would make believe that all his horses were kickers, just to keep us out of his stable. He wouldn't let us take his dogs for walks."

" What a hateful person he would be. I should never marry such a heartless monster as that, Fluff."

" Oh yes you would, if you liked him. You wouldn't mind how he trampled on us. Girls are so queer. Sarah's young man quarrelled with her one Sunday evening because she asked him to give her back half a sovereign that he'd borrowed off her."

"Borrowed off—oh, Fluff, what English! I won't hear another word about Sarah."

"And he was ever so rude to her; and she vowed she'd never walk out with him again; but she did, on her very next Sunday. They went to Hyde Park, and he treated her to curds and whey and seedy biscuits; so you see what fools girls are," gabbled Fluff, breathless in his obstinate eagerness to finish his story and point his moral.

"You must not talk of servants."

"What am I to talk of, then? There's nothing else in Palatine Square. I don't often see ladies and gentlemen, except mother and father; and they're always in a hurry."

There was a pause. Dora went on with her book, a romance of Italian life written by an American, a kind of novel that took a good deal of reading; and Fluff meditated.

"Is Sir Henry Mandeville's cousin a nice man?" he asked.

He was pleasant enough three years ago."

" Haven't you seen him for three years ? "

"No. He went to India in the *Mount Everest*, with your Aunt Georgie and Sir Henry."

" Oh ! And is he never coming back again ? "

" I dare say he will come back some day. Everybody comes back nowadays. India doesn't seem half so far away as it did when I was a child."

" He is sure to come back," pronounced Fluff, " unless he dies in India. But it's very likely he may die. There are tigers and snakes and mun-gooses—so that even a man who doesn't fight can get himself killed," with obvious contempt for the civilian.

" The mungoose is supposed to kill snakes, Fluff, not human beings."

" Bags I a mungoose, then, if ever I go to India. But I say, Aunt Dora, what's a civilian ? What kind of work does Sir Henry's cousin do ? "

" He is a civil engineer."

" What's that ? "

" A man who makes railroads, and waterworks,

and harbours like that," answered Dora, waving her sunshade in the direction of the pier, where a big excursion boat, with two funnels, was discharging her load of humanity, while another boat, almost as large and as crowded, was puffing itself hoarse in a passion of impatience just outside the harbour, waiting for her turn to come in.

"What! Does he dig, and work with a pickaxe, like a navvy?"

"No, dear, his work is chiefly with pen and ink."

"Ah, that's just what Stacie said. Civilians are poor creatures. They sit on stools with pens behind their ears."

"Perhaps some day you will see Sir Henry's cousin; and then you may not think him a poor creature."

"I don't want to see him—not never," exclaimed Fluff, with an emphatic double negative.

This was the end of Fluff's string of questions; and he speedily forgot all about Sir Henry Mandeville's cousin and Dora's blushes. Life was so full of action and variety in Imperial Crescent; and Fluff, in spite of his contempt for girls and pat-ball, found himself sucked into a whirlpool of Thomsons—the family next door but one—a family of six daughters and three sons, who owned an over-worked Q.C. for parent, and whose mother had retired from this life some years since, after having conscientiously filled her nursery. Mr. Thomson, Q.C., knew Mr. and Mrs. Lerwick in London, where he was occasionally seen boring himself at evening parties ; so the Lerwicks had been duly accredited to the Thomsons, and the two families had become almost as one.

An elderly governess had taken up the reins dropped by the worn-out mother, and the Thomson family scrambled on somehow under her fostering care. She was very kind to them. She looked after their clothes and ordered their food, and did battle with the servants, and took care that there was comfort of a sort, and a well-cooked dinner, for the bread-winner when he came flying down from Paper Buildings to visit his flock.

The eldest boy was three years older than Stacie, and the youngest was six months younger than Fluff, and allowed himself to be patronized

by that precocious person.   He had enjoyed none
of Fluff's London advantages, and had never had
such a guide, philosopher, and friend as Tandy
the groom.

In this juvenile society, in childish cricket
matches, in picnics on the solitary shore between
Pegwell and Sandwich, in excursions to see the
golfers on the links beyond that old-world town,
the summer days ran merrily on, and every new
day deepened the glow of health on Fluff's cheeks,
and gave fresh lustre to his bold blue eye.   Fluff,
who had crept about the low, hot London rooms,
pallid and dull, and heavy of limb, had now
almost as much vigour and elasticity of movement
as Pincher, whom he loved to race up and down
the green enclosure, or across the fields towards
St. Lawrence.

Never another thought gave Fluff to those
dim possibilities of his Aunt's marriage which had
been suggested to his young mind by those un-
accountable blushes of hers—never a thought, till,
sitting on the "Prom" one afternoon at Dora's

elbow, reading " The Children of the New Forest," for the eleventh time, with his legs stretched out along the bench, and his head and shoulders in his Aunt's lap, he heard a voice above him saying—

" I hope you have not quite forgotten me, Miss Hampden?"

He felt a tremor of surprise go through the slender figure against which he was leaning; and then Dora's voice answered in tones as tranquil as that strange voice above her.

"Oh no, I have not forgotten you, Mr. Doyle. I could hardly do that in three years; but it is rather startling to see you here. I thought you were in India."

"So I was till a month ago. I am home on leave."

" How nice for you ! "

"Yes; it is nice to come home and—see old friends again."

Evidently this was the Hindustani - talking cousin. Fluff dropped his legs off the bench in his astonishment, but he had not meant to make

L

room for the cousin, who seated himself, with prompt audacity, where Fluff's legs had been.

Fluff remained wedged between his aunt and the stranger, and surveyed the intruder with a most deliberate stare.

He was tall and broad-shouldered, and Fluff thought that the common herd might consider him good-looking. Fluff did not esteem himself a judge of so rough and manly a style. His ideal was a fairer and more delicate type—the face which he saw in the looking-glass when Miss Perry parted his hair, and which he had so often heard praised by his mother's friends. But for a roughish person the stranger was no doubt more than passable. Fluff liked the shape of his moustache, and the cut of his grey tweed suit. His boots left nothing to be desired.

Aunt Dora, who was usually bright and animated, had become curiously silent; and even the stranger, though he was bold as brass, seemed to have very little to say. He amused himself scraping hieroglyphics on the ground, with the point of his stick, for at least three minutes, before either he or the little Auntie found anything to say to each other.

"Did you see anything of Sir Henry and Georgie lately?" Dora inquired at last, as timidly as if she were taking a tremendous liberty in asking about her own people.

"I spent a week with them in the hills just before I left."

"And was my sister very well?"

"Very well, and very happy. The baby is tremendous. He is supposed in his own family circle to be the finest infant ever seen at Naini Tal. He gives a tea-party every afternoon."

"Skittles!" exclaimed Fluff, indignantly; "a baby can't give a party."

"Well, the tea-party may be nominally his mother's affair—but it's the baby that people come to see, and they are seldom let off seeing him."

"He is my godson," said Dora; and then the conversation flagged again, and Fluff began to entertain a very poor opinion of the Anglo-Indian intellect.

He thought better of the stranger by-and-by;

when he came to afternoon tea in the Crescent, and made himself agreeable to Miss Perry, Miss Mewk, the Thomson governess, and three Thomson girls, and incidentally revealed a respectable knowledge of cricket and the famous players thereof.

The three Miss Thomsons—the eldest of whom was almost grown up—thought him delightful. His coming gave a new zest to everybody's life, and had certainly brought a deepened rose-bloom to Aunt Dora's cheeks—a fact unpleasantly commented upon by Fluff in the broad publicity of the circular tea-table at which they were all seated, five-o'clock tea in the Crescent being a solid, business-like meal.

"You're blushing again, Auntie, just as you did that day you talked Hindustani," began Fluff. "She always blushes when she talks about India —Mr.—Mr.! Why, here we all are at tea, and we don't even know your name," he exclaimed, suddenly awakened to the absurdity of the situation.

"It's my fault," said Dora, confusedly; "I

ought to have introduced you all to Mr. Doyle—before we began tea. That is Eustace, Mr. Doyle, and this is Paul, and this little foolish boy is Frederick—sometimes called Fritz, and generally called Fluff."

"Oh, you are Fluff, are you?" asked Mr. Doyle. "You are the spoilt one. I have heard your Aunt Georgie talk about you."

"My Aunt Georgie can mind her own business," retorted Fluff, becoming as red as a turkey-cock. "She had better look after her own baby——"

"And spoil him just as your mother spoils you. Quite right, Fluff. She has begun the process already. He squalls loud enough to split the roof of the bungalow, if he doesn't get what he wants."

Fluff nursed his anger at the new-comer's insolence for at least five minutes—but that sunny room with three French windows open wide to the blue summer sea, the scent of the roses in the balcony, the loaded tea-table with piles of freshly-baked scones, a sultana cake in good cut, and stacks of jam sandwiches, and the animated faces of the three Miss Thomsons, and above all the

little Auntie's gentle influence, which always seemed
to harmonize everything, made against anger; so
Fluff pocketed the affront, and took another slice
of cake.

After tea the whole party set out for a walk to
Pegwell Bay, and this was the first of many such
walks that the two families took with Clement
Doyle as their leader.

The boys found out very soon that, however
they started upon their journey—even if Doyle led
the van, while Aunt Dora brought up the rear—it
happened somehow that before they were half-way
towards their destination Clement Doyle and Dora
Hampden were walking side by side.   There were
times when it seemed as if the little Auntie tried
hard to evade this companionship.   She would
fence herself in with a nephew on either side, and
a Thomson girl marching in front of her, and
Pincher skirmishing riotously round and round the
group—and yet somehow five minutes afterwards
she would be walking a little way in the rear of
the party alone with Clement Doyle.   It must
have been his experience as an engineer which

enabled him to circumvent every manœuvre of Aunt Dora and her nephews, who would insist before starting that she should not walk with Mr. Doyle.

"You are not *his* aunt," Fluff urged indignantly. "He has no business to take you away from us."

"No!" assented Eustace moodily; "but I'm afraid he will take her away some day—take her out to the Punjaub, or somewhere equally horrid, to live among the blacks."

Paul, who never lost a chance of improving his elder brother, hastened to assure him that the inhabitants of the Punjaub were only a pale copper colour.

"They're not white, at any rate—and Aunt Dora had much better stop among people of her own complexion."

"She ain't going to India!" protested Fluff, stamping his foot. "She's going to stay with us, always—always—always."

He finished with a burst of passionate tears as Aunt Dora came into the room dressed for walking; and just at that moment Clement Doyle appeared at the French window with a whole troop of Thomsons at his heels. He had contrived to get lodgings in the Crescent, and seemed to be always in the garden, within call of the Lerwicks and Thomsons, when he was not in the Lerwick drawing-room.

"Auntie, you are not to go to India!" screamed Fluff, as the lady entered by the door and the gentleman appeared at the window. "You are not to go. You're to be our Auntie always, and take care of us when Mother's too busy with her parties and things. Mother says you are never going to marry—and if you do go and get married and go to India it will be downright cheating."

This time the colour in Aunt Dora's cheeks was like the crimson peony rather than the rose.

"Shut up, you young booby," cried Paul. "Who said anything about Aunt going to India?"

"Stacie did. He said Mr. Doyle would take her to the Pun—something—all among the blacks. But she mustn't go. She belongs to us."

So far as any notice of this speech went the engineer might have been stone deaf. He was keenly interested in the appearance of a brig in full sail on the horizon, and was explaining every inch of her canvas to the Miss Thomsons.

The excursion on this particular occasion was to Richborough Castle, five miles by road, hugging the coast, and then across a sleepy little river in a ferry-boat, and then a "jolly" walk over the fields. Paul and Fluff were to ride their shelties as far as the ferry, sharing them occasionally with Charlie, the smallest of the Thomsons, who, not being costumed for riding, exhibited a good deal of wrinkled stocking and an occasional inch of bare leg below the saddle. Everybody else was to walk, including little Miss Perry, who was not so good at walking as Aunt Dora, and sometimes found herself wondering whether she realized the advantage of living with a "carriage family," when she was continually on the march.

CHAPTER X.

DORA PERCEIVES A DIVIDED DUTY.

TANDY had been sent in advance with the pony-cart and the lunch, a real picnic lunch—two baskets of substantial food, and a stone jar of ginger beer, and plenty of milk and methylated spirits for the afternoon tea. Everybody's mind had been brought to bear on those baskets; and the Miss Thomsons and Miss Perry recapitulated their contents as they trudged along the level road beyond Pegwell Bay, with the wide-stretching turnip fields, and oats and barley on their right, and the low marshes on their left, skirting a sea that in the foreground lay calm and smooth, a dull purple expanse, brightening towards the horizon into a long line of translucent green. And along this low, sandy shore the sea was so shallow that

Pincher, having started in pursuit of a gull, was able to run out ever so far, a flash of living whiteness across the dark grey water ; and Ramsgate, as they stopped to look back at it—the wooded cliffs on this side of Pegwell Bay, the higher cliffs beyond, dazzling white in the sun, the distant tower of the Granville, the windmill by the promenade—seemed just the one most enchanting place in the civilized world.

They passed the Sportsman—a little inn with a tea-garden—and Eustace wondered if it had any connection with the most interesting newspaper he knew of—that superior journal in which he had first seen his own name in print ; and after a walk which Miss Perry thought endless they came to a nice old roadside inn where, at the sign of the Red Lion, the ponies were taken possession of by an ostler, and the boys refreshed themselves with ginger beer and biscuits.

Next came the passage of the river Stour, in a roomy old boat which let in more water and mud than Miss Perry thought agreeable, though she stood on a bench with Aunt Dora, safe out of the

dirt, and with her slender form steadied by Mr.
Doyle's strong hand, while with his other hand
he sustained Aunt Dora. It was so narrow a
stream that the ferry was hardly worth speaking
about, and Eustace declared that the Elstree boy
who won the long jump would have cleared it
from bank to bank.

Before them, when they had landed, there
stretched a broad expanse of pasture, enclosed by
blind ditches, and tall five-barred gates, but to the
eye open as an Arabian desert.   Here in the deep
rich grass dark red cattle and pale grey sheep were
grazing in separate colonies ; and to keep these
flocks and herds in their proper pastures the big
gates were all jealously locked, and had to be
climbed ; a light and easy process for country-
bred Dora, a toilsome ordeal for Miss Perry, whose
gown, neat and unpretending enough, was not
tailor-made, and was far from "rational" when
considered in relation to five-barred gates.

There stood Richborough Castle in the distance,
on a rising ground that only courtesy could call a
hill, the cyclopean walls so clothed with ivy that

the ruin looked like a wood, and only here and there the grey stone showed pale against the dark green of that ivy curtain. A friendly woman came out of a cottage garden, gay with hollyhocks, to unlock the gates of the level crossing—the line running between those low pastures and the castle hill—and to unlock another gate that opened into a green lane under the walls : and if they had known of this good person's cottage they need have brought no apparatus for their picnic tea, as it was her delight to provide for visitors to the castle ; but any such convenient arrangement would have been far inferior to their own spirit-lamp and tea-kettle, in Fluff's opinion.

It was a real picnic. They had started soon after breakfast, and they were to spend the whole day on the walk to and fro, and within the old castle walls—such glorious walls for climbing, so broad and massive, and not alarmingly high, and with a picturesque break here and there. They found one such place just suited for spreading a table-cloth—dazzling white in the sun—and setting out a homely feast ; a niche for everybody's feet, a comfortable stone for everybody to sit upon, the countryside, the placid, simple, rural home-life of old England lying in summer stillness all around them, save yonder on the horizon where, blue and beautiful, stretched the summer sea, the watery way to everywhere.

"Is that the way you would go to India?" Fluff asked Clement Doyle, pointing to the sea-line, silvery in the vivid light.

"Yes, Fluff; my ship would pass right in front of your windows, if I sailed from Tilbury in a P. and O."

"We'll look for you when you are passing, and you might wave your handkerchief—if we are still at Ramsgate when you go."

"I am not going back just yet, Fluff; not for a year."

"What long holidays you get. Then we shan't be in the Crescent when you go; unless Mother lets Auntie bring us to Ramsgate again next year. Auntie will always take us to the seaside, don't you know," said Fluff, with intention. "She will have to—because Mother can't."

"Oh, she will have to, will she?" asked Clement Doyle, slowly puffing at his pipe.

He and Fluff were sitting a little way from the rest, on an angle of the old wall, half buried in the ivy, Doyle having withdrawn to smoke, and Fluff having clambered after him to the green sanctuary.

"Yes, she'll have to take us wherever we go," repeated Fluff, very seriously. "We've got other aunts, but she's the only aunt we care for; and she means never, never, never to marry anybody, so that she can always take care of us."

"Oh, is that what she means? And when you are all grown up and married, and have children of your own to look after—what will become of your little Auntie then?"

"Oh, she'll be awfully old then—and she'll be quite happy—with a Nangora cat—and Pincher— no, he'll be dead — another dog azackly like Pincher, perhaps his great-grandson—and a nice house by the sea where we can all go and stop with her every summer."

"And after taking care of you while she's young,

she'll have nobody to take care of her when she's getting elderly."

"We shall all take care of her. I'm never going to marry. I hate girls. Those Thomsons are enough to sicken anybody. And perhaps," concluded Fluff, condescendingly, "I shall live with her."

"Only perhaps," said Clement, gravely. "She is to spend all the best days of her life for you, on the strength of a perhaps. I suppose that is what women are meant for."

"Of course, they're meant to take care of children, and look after boys," assented Fluff; "and as Auntie is never going to marry—— "

"But why shouldn't she marry?"

"Nobody has ever asked her. She isn't pretty, like the others, you know."

"Indeed I don't know."

"Perhaps you think her pretty," Fluff said, with a shade of contempt in his voice. "You see, you're only accustomed to Indian women."

"I think she has something better than mere prettiness, Fluff," the engineer answered, gravely. "I think she has the sweetest face in the world,

and the sweetest nature ; and that you must be a
very selfish little boy if you don't wish for her
happiness more than for your own convenience in
having a nice little Aunt always at your beck and
call."

Here a whole bevy of Thomsons, shrieking and
giggling as they clambered and stumbled over the
ivy-covered stones, put a stop to confidential talk ;
but Fluff pondered seriously upon all that Clement
Doyle had said, and he felt that there was something bad behind. He had suspected Sir Henry's
cousin from the first mention of his name ; and
now that cousin was beginning to show the cloven
foot in real earnest. Fluff thought still worse of
Clement Doyle half an hour later when, after in-
augurating a game at hide-and-seek, which
absorbed all the juvenile party, and even Miss
Perry, he was descried suddenly in the distance
strolling away towards Sandwich with Dora.
They had vanished almost as silently as the world-
famous Boojum.

They came back to tea, and Fluff, who was as
good at listening and watching as if he had been

training for the detective police, noticed a change in his aunt's manner—a change from that bright intelligence and deftness of hand, which enabled her to do everything better than everybody else, to absolute helplessness. She could not even make the kettle boil. The methylated spirit was too much for her. The thin flames were blown about under the kettle in a most futile way, till Clement Doyle took the business in hand and engineered it through. She, who was usually the Princess of tea-makers, blundered with the teapot; and she, who could cut the most enticing knobs and hunches of bread-and-butter—crusty pieces that would have tempted an anchorite—to-day could hardly butter a halfpenny bun.

Her wits had gone wool-gathering. Her fingers had lost their cunning. She gave Fluff a sudden hug in the middle of tea, and he felt a tear drop upon his forehead as she drew his childish head to her breast, and for the rest of the meal she sat very still and silent, looking dreamily across the level flats to the distant sea, where the ships had golden sails in the westering sun.

If the six-year-old Fluff was able to note this change in his aunt's demeanour, it was not likely that it would escape the shrewd eyes of Stacie and Paul, although these two were more occupied by the Thomson girls and boys than their small brother. They were hungry, too, and flushed by the excitement of the games they had been playing. They felt that there was some new fever in the air; and when they crossed the fields in the cool eventide, an hour after tea, Stacie was hardly surprised at his aunt's putting her arm through his and asking him to walk with her.

"Wouldn't you rather walk with Doyle?" asked Stacie, maliciously. "It generally comes to that, you know, before we've gone very far."

Good-natured as Stacie was, he could not spare her this stab. They were all of them jealous of Clement Doyle. The Father of the Faithful could not be more anxious to keep his favourite Sultana under lock and key than these three nephews were to keep their aunt all to themselves.

"No, dear, I want to walk with you, and only you. Mr. Doyle can look after the young ones."

"Like an usher," laughed Stacie. "That's about all he's fit for."

"I want to tell you something, dear," Dora said, softly, when they had crossed the Stour, and the party was well under weigh upon the road to Ramsgate, the Thomsons and Pincher ahead with Doyle, Paul and Fluff raising a prodigious dust on their shelties, and Miss Perry in the pony-cart with Tandy and the empty jars and baskets. They were carrying home nothing but empties; for the gipsies, who haunt such places, had cleared out all their leavings, and gipsy babies had choked themselves with their surplus buns.

"If it's anything about Doyle, I don't want to hear it," said Stacie, sternly.

He prided himself upon dropping the "Mr." and talking of the engineer as "Doyle." It was his assertion of manhood.

"It is about myself, Stacie, and Mr. Doyle."

"Oh, of course! He has talked you into getting yourself engaged to him. Fluff was right. He saw through the fellow all along. Paul and I were too green."

"Stacie, it isn't kind or nice of you to talk like that."

"Ain't it? Well, it isn't kind or nice of you to go and get yourself engaged to the first bounder who asks you to marry him."

"It is very shameful of you to call him that insulting name," remonstrated Dora, who had but the vaguest notion of what the obnoxious word meant.

She knew only that her nephews applied it in contumely to almost everybody of the male sex.

They walked on a little while in silence, and then Dora said half tearfully, "If you are going to be rude, Stacie, and if you are not interested in my happiness, I won't tell you anything more."

"Of course I want you to be happy; but why can't you go on being happy with us? What do you want with a duffer like that coming in upon us to spoil everything? We all doat upon you, and when we are grown up and come into our fortunes, there's nothing in the world we won't give you. If you want a yacht, you can have it, directly I come of age—a schooner, with auxiliary steam; and I shall keep race-horses, not such crocks as father's; and I'll take you to Newmarket and Doncaster; and to Monte Carlo every winter; and to Nice for the Carnival. I should study you in everything. And why spoil it all for an oiler like that? It's maddening."

"Eustace! If you go on calling him low vulgar names, I'll never speak to you again."

"Oh! I'll call him a duke if you like. I shan't hate him any less. Why you should go and get yourself engaged to him is more than I can understand. For I suppose you are engaged to him?"

"Yes, dear. He asked me to be his wife—this afternoon. He is going to write to your grandfather to-night, and if my father consents——"

"Oh! he'll consent fast enough; fathers always do. I shouldn't like to ask Mr. Thomson for one of his daughters when I'm grown up. I should be afraid he'd offer me three."

"But I hope you know, Stacie, that being engaged won't make the least difference in my love for you and your brothers."

"Only the difference of from here to the

Punjaub; for I suppose you'll have to go to India
with him. He's got to get his living in India, and
you'll have to go and keep house for him; and no
doubt you'll think yourself happy when there
isn't a panther in your garden—compound, those
asses call it—or a cobra under your pillow, or
millions of red ants eating your furniture. Perhaps you like the idea of living in the Zoological
Gardens, with the temperature of the palm-house
at Kew?"

"I don't like the idea of leaving you and your
brothers, Stacie."

"Gammon! If you wanted to stay with us, you
wouldn't promise to go with him," said Eustace;
and even to Dorothea's mind there was stern logic
in this bitter speech.

She was making her choice in life. It must
needs be that she loved her newly-betrothed better
than father, and sisters, and nephews; better than
these boys to whom she had given the best part
of her thoughts and of her heart hitherto. She
was a deserter; and she felt herself called up for
judgment before this thirteen-year-old nephew, and

found guilty, without extenuating circumstances. She had loved these boys because they had need of her love. With all the advantages that wealth could give they had wanted much that the children of parents in far humbler circumstances generally reckon upon with as great a certainty as upon the air they breathe. They had lacked a father's thoughtful supervision, a mother's watchful care. They had been loved after a fashion—as lap-dogs and birds in cages are loved—cherished tenderly one day, almost forgotten the next. Foolish indulgence had been lavished upon them. They had been trained to consider luxuries as absolute necessities. They were tired of things of which the briefest possession would have filled middle-class boys with rapture.

Dora had seen how all the best things in life were lacking to these children. She had tried in her own gentle way to awaken her sister to a sense of maternal duty, and she had even talked seriously to Mr. Lerwick, who heard her with delightful good temper, and laughed off her suggestions in the pleasantest way possible. He knew he was a careless beggar, and didn't lecture his boys as he ought; but in a few years they'd be old enough to lecture him, and take care of him. They'd never have to work for their living. That was one comfort.

Dora found how hopeless it is to argue with a pair of feather-headed people who think that pleasure and idleness are the chief good in life. Father and mother were both amiable and well-meaning; but the idea of parental duty had never shaped itself in the mind of either parent. To be indulgent, to lavish gifts, constituted their ideal of parental affection. And seeing these things, Dora told herself that it was her duty to make up the sum of thoughtful love which was deficient in her sister's household. Since the birth of her youngest nephew she had spent nearly half her life in her sister's nursery. She had gladly accepted the office of spinster-aunt, and had asked nothing better of fate than to be loved by her sister's children. She had been taught to think herself an unattractive little person, had been accustomed to hear herself compared disparagingly with her handsome sisters, and had made up her mind that all the sweet trouble and confusion of a love-affair, all the fuss and flutter of a trousseau and wedding gown, were to be a dead letter for her. Nobody would ever care for the poor little plain sister; and nobody should ever see that the poor little plain sister was sorry for her fate. She made up her mind that she was to be an old maid; and having settled this with herself once and for ever, as she thought, she became by far the brightest and gayest and most even-tempered of the Hampden sisters.

And then one fine summer day, like the vision of a sunlit glade in an enchanted forest, there had opened before her a new vista of life, a new view of the world in which her lot was cast. She had discovered suddenly that she, too, might be loved. This clever good man, successful in his profession, popular in his family, a man with excellent prospects in life—nay, every chance of a distinguished career—cared for her as much as if she had been the handsomest of her sisters; Georgiana even, the flower of the flock, with whom

he had ample opportunity for comparing her insignificant person.

Very little had been said in those golden days
at Mill Park, and then after the honeymoon
Clement Doyle had accompanied Sir Henry and
Lady Mandeville to India; but before he left he
had made a special journey to Devonshire, and
had come over from the new hotel at Bideford
one morning as if he had dropped from the clouds,
and had startled Dorothea in the midst of a
morning walk with her dogs. She was the last of
the sisters; and the highly-accomplished finishing
governess, whose chief conversation was about
frocks and hats and the neighbouring gentry, had
been paid off. So Dora had only the dogs for
company. Her father was one of those rural
squires who might as well have been born on four
legs; since the only use they ever make of two is
to take them to their parish church on Sunday
mornings. Dora hardly knew what it was to go
for a walk with her father.

Clement Doyle had come to Devonshire ex-
pressly to bid her good-bye, and to ask her if she

would wait for him. That was all he had asked.
Would she wait for three or four years, till he
could come back to claim her? He had an important work to finish in Upper India, and the
life he would have to lead under canvas while that
work was in progress was a rougher life than he
would like to share with his young wife.

If she should wait for him?

If! She had but to look in his face with those
earnest eyes of hers, and lay her hand in his, for
him to know that she would wait a lifetime.

And so they had parted, that October morning,
between the tall hedgerows where the berries were
reddening for the ravenous winter birds, within the
sound of the sea that rolls up to Bideford Bay.
So they had parted, not absolutely engaged; only
waiting for each other. Nobody had been told
anything. Dorothea had kept her little secret.
The lovers had only written to each other at long
intervals, and the letters that passed between
them were hardly love-letters. But now this day,
between Richborough and the sea, the promise of
three years ago had been ratified by another

promise: the promise of two lives that were to be as one.

Dora and Eustace had walked on for nearly ten minutes in silence before the boy discovered that his aunt was crying.

"Come, come, little Auntie, that won't do," he exclaimed, melted in a moment at the sight of those tears. "You mustn't cry. I was a beastly selfish beggar to talk like that. Of course you must marry him if you like—only I wonder you do like. I can't see any particular points about him—though he is a good over-hand bowler," interjected Stacie, musingly, remembering a certain cricket match in which Mr. Doyle's services had been enlisted. "And if you think you'll be as happy in India as you have been in England—of course you must do what you like. I was a rude beast to rag you about getting engaged. Why," —with a sudden touch of scorn—"Perry will be getting herself engaged next—or old Warren."

"Does it seem so very strange, Stacie, that any one should care about me?"

"No, no; I didn't mean that. Only I didn't

think you were the marrying sort. Well, I shall be at Harrow next year, and I shall be out of it. You won't be married yet awhile, I suppose?"

"I hope not for a year, Stacie."

"You hope not! You can do as you like about it, can't you? He's not going to tyrannise over you before you're married."

"I don't think he will ever be a tyrant, dear."

"Don't you? All engaged girls think their geese are swans. . I know it was sickening to hear Aunt Georgie talk about Sir Henry when they were staying at Heatherside before they were married; and still more sickening to see the way she waited upon him, and mended his gloves, and fussed when he cut his finger."

"I promise not to make a fuss about my sweetheart, unless he is seriously hurt. And you will try to like Clement, won't you, Stacie, for my sake?"

"Clement! Are you going to call him Clement?"

"I think he would like me to do so."

"Oh, you are going to be a regular engaged

couple, I see. There'll be no end of spooning.
As to liking him, we all like him well enough;
but we don't like his sneaking after you. And if
we come to Ramsgate next year, you won't be
with us. We shall have old Warren, perhaps,
instead—somebody Mother can trust. It'll be
beastly slow. I think I'd rather spend the vac.
in London, and do a round of the theatres in the
front row of the pit, with Tandy. And he *can*
shove. He'd be worth his place as a forward, if
he only had the weight."

"Oh, you must have your seaside holiday,
dear. Perhaps I may not be married till after
next summer—or if I am, Mother would bring
you."

"Catch her! She won't leave Palatine Square
till after Goodwood, and after Goodwood she'll be
going off to Homburg for her cure. She ain't the
least little bit ill, but directly the London parties
are all over, her doctor tells her she wants tone.
Then off she goes to Homburg, with four American
trunks, and she dines on the Kursaal Terrace
every night among military bands and fireworks,

and we are sent to Heatherside with old Warren
to look after us."

Aunt Dora rebuked Stacie for this rude mention
of this worthy lady, and he promised to call her
Miss Warren in future, whenever he could think
of it.

"The other comes much more natural," he said,
apologetically.

"I can't think how it is that vulgarity comes
naturally to all schoolboys, whether they live in
Palatine Square or in Camberwell. I'm sure the
Camberwell boys can't be any worse than you."

"Oh, can't they? You should hear 'em, Auntie.
We played against a cad-eleven once, and you
should have heard 'em ask 'for the toime,' and
you should have seen 'em eat, and the warts on
their hands. I think those boys beat the record
for warts."

Dora preached a little sermon about the responsibilities of boys whose parents give them everything in the world they want. She also told him
how many of England's greatest men had begun
their lives in just such seminaries as those which

he called cad-schools ; and how the boys and men most to be respected were those who did most for themselves, and owed very little to their parents.

He heard her politely, but was hardly convinced.

"I'm afraid you're a horrid little Rad, Auntie, in spite of your Primrose brooch," he said. "Is Doyle a Rad, too?"

"No, dear. He's a Unionist."

"Ah, that's worse—so beastly middle-class."

"He used to work in one of the University Missions before he went to India, and he is thoroughly in touch with the working classes."

"Is he? Then I hope he don't mind their dirty hands."

"His knowledge of the poor has been of great use to him in his up-country work, for though an English workman and a low-class Hindoo are very different, they are both human beings, and they have some things in common, and Clement has been able to attach those poor creatures to him, and to get their very best work out of them."

"Ah, he stuffs you up with all his fine doings, no doubt."

"No, Stacie. It was Aunt Georgie who told me about him."

"Ah! Aunt Georgie is like the fox in the fable. She's got to be broiled alive in India herself; and she'd like you to go out and be cooked in the same oven."

They were near Pegwell Bay by this time, and Clement Doyle dropped back a little, and joined Dora and her nephew; and Stacie, feeling somewhat conscience-stricken at the thought of his harshness to the best of aunts, ran on to overtake the Thomsons, and left Dora and her lover to a *tête-à-tête*. No doubt, in spite of all their talk this afternoon along the grassy levels by the sea, in a Paul Potter landscape, where the drowsy cattle never lifted their heads to look at them, these happy lovers had worlds to say to each other this evening, if it were only to expatiate upon the splendour of the sunset.

CHAPTER XI.

MAKING THE BEST OF IT.

"So she married the barber," cried Stacie, in his boyish voice, as he ran out on to the Imperial lawn next morning before breakfast, and discovered his Aunt Dora pacing slowly in front of the dining-room windows with Clement Doyle at her side. "So she married the barber, at St. James's, Piccadilly; and the wedding presents were on view with tea and buns all the afternoon in Palatine Square; and the grand Panjandrum didn't come to the wedding—because the barber wasn't in his set, you see."

These were Stacie's morning spirits. Life seemed so lovely upon that breezy height, with summer wavelets scarcely crisped in the soft west wind, and with the curving coast between

Ramsgate and Deal wrapped in cool shadow, the presage of fine weather. A fine healthy boy couldn't feel sorry about anything on such a morning as this; and Stacie had the happiest disposition and the warmest heart among the three brothers.

Clement Doyle clapped a friendly hand on his shoulder.

"Well, youngster, what's the matter with you?"

"Nothing's the matter—at least, nothing that can be helped now. Only I should like to have everything fair and square, don't you know, about you and the little Auntie, before——"

"Before you give your consent?" laughed Doyle.

"Eg-zackly," replied Stacie, with a pause between the syllables; "I dare say you think that I and my brothers have no right to be consulted; but we just have, you see; because, before you came sneaking along——"

"Oh, Stacie!"

"Let him talk, Dora. He means no harm. I know the vocabulary."

"Auntie belonged to us. She had only a fusty old father down in Devonshire."

"Eustace!"

"She didn't even pretend to care about him," pursued Stacie, deaf to remonstrances. "She had only us, and she doted on us—didn't you now, little Auntie?"

"No more than I do now, dearest."

"Fudge! If I brought home a Dandy Dinmont do you think Pincher would believe I cared as much about *him* as I did when he was my only dog? And do you expect me to have less gumption than a fox-terrier? No, Aunt Dora, you have gone and got yourself engaged. It's a chouse for us; but you've done it; and we had better look the business straight in the face."

And then turning to Clement Doyle, he asked with his most completely grown-up air, "When do you mean to get married, you two?"

"I mean what your Aunt means, Eustace. Our wedding-day can't come too soon for me. I should like to be married next October, and to take my wife for a long honeymoon by the Mediterranean."

"She'll have enough of the Mediterranean when you're taking her to India, to be baked as black as a coal," said Stacie. "I wonder you can have the impudence to talk about next October."

"Don't excite yourself, dear," pleaded Dora, putting a caressing arm round her nephew's neck. He was only two or three inches shorter than the little Auntie. "I am not going to break my word. I am not going to be married till my nephews are a year older. And when you are at Harrow, Stacie, you won't care about being petted and looked after by an aunt."

"Oh yes I shall. I shall like the rough-and-tumble at school; but when I have had a bone broken at footer, who will there be to nurse me at home?"

"Well, there'd be your mother," said Doyle.

"Mother! She'd go into hysterics at sight of broken bones, and forget all about them next morning. The little Auntie is the only relation we have who knows what's the matter with us when we're ill, or the kind of things we like when we're well. Don't make any mistake about it,

Mr. Doyle. You are going to take away just the one person we want."

"I'm sorry your affections haven't a wider range. But a year is a long time; and when I do take your aunt away I hope it won't be for ever, or for many years. We shall come back soon enough to visit you at Oxford when you are an undergrad, perhaps. I suppose it will be the House, and the Bullingdon Club, for you oof-birds."

"It'll be the House, of course. And I hope they'll elect me for the Bullingdon. Well, you are to be married October twelve months, or thereabouts; at the worst, not before the end of August, next year."

"I don't know if my extension of leave will stretch to that, Stacie—they may want to begin the new railway in June, and if so, I shall have to go in May."

"If you have, you must go alone, then. She said she wasn't going to marry for at least a year, and she'll have to keep her word."

"There's the gong for breakfast sounding a second time, and there's Miss Perry on the look-out for you," said Doyle. "I suppose you won't grudge me a cup of tea and a slice of bread-and-jam, if I join you at breakfast?"

"Auntie is the mistress of the house."

Dora's sweetheart went into the dining-room with them, and dropped into a chair on Dora's side of the table, a seat which he occupied at so many meals as the summer days went by, that it soon came to be known as his place, and no one else ever tried to appropriate it. He was rarely privileged to sit quite next to Dora, as Fluff put in a claim to the place on her right hand, and squeezed himself resolutely between her and her future husband, while Stacie claimed to sit on her left. Paul, as being learned and self-sufficient, was left out in the cold, and lectured them all from the opposite side of the table, where he sat next Miss Perry, who was enchanted with the novel aspect of things, and took the keenest interest in the lovers. She was of a mild and retiring disposition, which is peculiarly adapted to looking on at the drama of life. She had never had a sweetheart of her own; but she had fed her young

fancy upon the most sentimental novels; and it
was a delight to her to sit on the remotest window-
seat, absorbed in a satin-stitch tea-cloth, while
the lovers talked together in confidential murmur-
ings, of which only an occasional sentence reached
her ear.

CHAPTER XII.

MRS. LERWICK PHILOSOPHIZES.

MRS. LERWICK came down to Imperial Crescent on a flying visit, just before starting for Marienbad for her cure, while her husband went to Royat for his cure—it being an essential point among really "smart" people that the husband and wife should never go to the same place to be cured. It is only the dowdy couples, the Darbys and Joans, who creep about the same health resort, and sit side by side day after day at the same *table d'hôte*.

Mrs. Lerwick was in despair at the idea of Dora's engagement, and was inclined to be indignant with her youngest sister for contemplating marriage, though she did not express herself quite as frankly as her sons.

"You are the last person I should have thought

of marrying, and he is the last person I should have thought you would like," she said.

"Do you consider him such a very disagreeable person?" Dora asked, with a wounded air.

"Oh dear no; I think him most agreeable— quite a striking personality—but not a bit your style."

"What do you think my style would be, Nell?"

"Oh, something very different: a churchy person —a clergyman, perhaps—and a good deal older than yourself—middle-aged, and thoughtful, and —and—rather short—some one more like Mr. Bolger."

Bolger was a senior curate who had been silently devoted to Dora in her earliest girlhood, had hung about her in the schools, and had insisted on lending her his favourite books—books that were far too dry for her youthful taste. Dora had been chaffed about Bolger, and Bolger's attentions had been held up to contempt and ridicule, and Bolger's person and manners had been treated as a joke by the whole of the Hampden family; and now it was a hard thing for Dora to be told that a person resembling Mr. Bolger would be her style.

"I see you think Clement a great deal too good for me," she said, with a faint little laugh.

"Oh dear no, not too good. He is very handsome certainly, and I dare say you'll find him a bit of a flirt in India; but you have read Rudyard Kipling's stories, and you know what you've got to expect. Oh no, dear, he is not too good for you. Father wrote and told me you and he will be just comfortably off—you'll have bread-and-cheese to start with. And then by-and-by he may get on, and get a really fine appointment. I hear there are great openings for an engineer who has made a little bit of a name for himself, as Mr. Doyle has; and altogether I congratulate you, darling."

Mrs. Lerwick punctuated her congratulations with a kiss.

"How do you like my hat?" she asked, parenthetically. "It's the new shape."

"It's very pretty. But is it really different from the last?"

"Really different? Why, it's an utterly new style. They haven't a curve in common. Yes, dear, I congratulate you—but I'm very sorry for the boys. They'll miss you woefully."

"Not if you give them a little more of your time, Nell. I dare say you will be going out less as you get older."

"Less! Why, of course, I shall be going out ever so much more every year of my life. We know more people every season, don't you know —and better people. Indeed, we are gradually getting into a really nice set—a set that it pays one to entertain thoroughly well; even if one doesn't get very intimate with them. Of course, I don't pretend to be a leader. Nobody less than a Peeress can be that. But still people have talked about me, and about my frocks; and— and—Belle puts me among the pretty people; and the flowers at my last evening party were described in all the really good society papers. In fact, as Tony says, we are beginning to catch on."

The phrase was Hebrew to Dora. She could

only open her pretty grey eyes a little wider, and wait for her loquacious sister to draw breath.

"We are getting to count among the really smart people, and goodness knows what mayn't happen next year. I am inclined to think that Tony ought to go into the House. Not that there's any distinction in that nowadays; but it brings a man shoulder to shoulder with important people. And Tony is a staunch Conservative, though he knows absolutely nothing about politics."

"And the boys—are they never to see anything of you?" asked Dora, despairingly. "Are they to know less and less of their father and mother as the years go on?"

"Don't gush, Dora! You are so absurdly senti-mental. The boys will be at school and at the 'Varsity for the next ten years; and that is just the time in which Tony and I can enjoy ourselves, and occupy a proper place in society. When Eustace leaves Oxford he will be able to go to parties with me—and we shall be inseparable. I dare say I shall have given up waltzing by that time; though I may sometimes stand up in a square—with extra nice people," concluded Mrs. Lerwick, having a vision of Royalties gliding gracefully through a condescending quadrille.

Dora's spirits sank very low after this conversation with her sister. It was to such a mother as this, and to a father who was a nullity, that she was to leave the boys she loved. She was to leave them with their minds unformed, their characters waiting for the moulder's hand, fortified and braced by no better influence than the schoolboy's elastic code of honour—truth and loyalty to pals, anything to masters. She was to leave them in a home where religious influences were limited to Sunday morning service at a fashionable and overcrowded church. She was to leave them to the hazard of hired teachers, the chance of finding good or evil guides. She was to leave them amidst the worst possible surroundings—a luxurious home, ruled for the most part by servants.

She had given Clement Doyle her promise; and what woman who at the mature age of seven-and-twenty loves and is fondly loved again can break the promise given to her first lover? She would have made any sacrifice for her nephews, except the sacrifice of the man who was far dearer to her than herself. And yet in the midst of her happiness this cloud of fear for Ellinor Lerwick's children hung heavily over her. She tried to hope that the mother's better nature would develop as time went on, that satiety would come even in Palatine Square, that no woman could go on dancing and dressing and gadding from one gaudy scene to another, season after season, and not find the hollowness in the drum, the dust and ashes at the core of the golden fruit. Satiety must come by-and-by, and her sister's heart and mind would be awakened to the knowledge of those better and sweeter pleasures that women find who live most in their children's lives.

In the meantime there was a year—a whole year—in which to try and fortify these boys with the armour of manly honour and manly common sense, so that the evil example of frivolous parents and over-paid servants might pass them by, and leave them unspoilt, firm in good principles and right feeling, and able to understand what are the really precious things of this life. There was time, perhaps, to draw them very near to her, to make them see as she saw and think as she thought, if she were but permitted to spend the greater portion of the year with them. It was in no self-sufficiency that she thought of herself as a good influence in her nephews' lives. She was not puffed up with any notion of her own superiority. She thought of herself only as one who had not been caught in the fly-wheel of the society machine, who had not been spoilt by riches or the flattery of foolish people, who stood outside all the temptations which had made Ellinor Lerwick the woman she was.

"There is no merit in my not caring for fashion and gaiety," she told herself. "They have never been within my reach."

She could count upon her father's willingness to let her spend as much of her life as she liked with her sister's children. He was a man who hunted three days a week, all through the hunting

O

season, and needed no amusement in the evening.
She would be allowed to spend her autumn at
Heatherside, and to have the boys at Mill Park
for their Christmas holidays. She was the mistress
of her own life. Mr. Hampden had not accustomed
himself to depend upon his daughters for society
or amusement. He had never encouraged them
to care for riding, lest they should take it into
their heads to want to hunt, and so lessen the
comfort of his own three days a week, or deprive
him of a second horse when he wanted one. He
had seen them marry and leave him, one after
another, without a pang; and though he wrote to
Clement Doyle of his "one ewe lamb," and affected
to give a regretful consent to Dora's engagement,
his satisfaction might be read between the lines
of his letter.

"My daughters have all married young, and
they have married gentlemen," he wrote. "I am
proud of my sons-in-law. And I am happy to
know that my youngest darling—my one ewe
lamb—has chosen as worthily as her elder sisters."

Dora, brooding over this letter, could not help

wondering what her father found to be proud of in Tony Lerwick, whose fortune had been made for him by his father and grandfather, and whose highest earthly ambition was to own a Derby winner.

CHAPTER XIII.

IN THE GOLDEN AUTUMN.

DURING the day and a half that she was able to spare for domesticity, Mrs. Lerwick arranged the future movements of her children, in her rather sketchy way. Her presence had a deteriorating influence upon Fluff, who had been as good as gold until her arrival, and who began to be naughty five minutes after she crossed the threshold. The only quiet time in Imperial Crescent was the evening hour after this exacting young person had gone to bed, under convoy of Miss Perry, and had been read to sleep with a half-hour fairy tale by Aunt Dora, who made it a point that no story she read to Fluff when his head was on the pillow should last more than half an hour. Knowing this, Fluff made a conscientious effort to fall asleep towards the end of the story, keeping very still, with his limbs lying loosely where they fell, and abstaining from all thought of to-morrow. Pittman had vainly urged that it was bad for little boys to have their minds "egzited" after they were in bed. Aunt Dora was always polite, but she was not in the habit of accepting Pittman's judgment about anything; and in long conversations below-stairs the nurse complained bitterly of the slights to which she was subjected, and asked what was the use of twenty years' experience with children, in the houses of the aristocracy, if her knowledge and experience were to be set at naught by a chit of a girl like Miss Hampden?

"But little Fritz have picked up wonderful since she come," pleaded Sarah; "and she do seem to have a clever head on her, and to manage those three unruly boys beautiful. To see the dinners they make, too—it's a pleasure to take 'em a second help of roast mutton."

"They eat a great deal too much," said nurse, sourly; "and I expect we shall have them all in the doctor's hands directly we get back to the Square."

"Not directly, nurse," said Sarah; "it'll take a fortnight of your management to bring 'em to that."

And then Sarah, whom nurse had hectored for tardy home-coming on her last evening out, laughed the laugh of scorn; and Tandy the groom, who was picking a casual bit of dinner at the indoor servants' table, chuckled audibly. Nurse Pittman was not a favourite. She had none of cook's large powers; and she gave herself more airs than cook, on the strength of doing less work.

Cook in Imperial Crescent, be it understood, was only kitchen-maid in Palatine Square, where her understudy, the vegetable-maid, was now assisting the *chef*, and qualifying to take service as a forty-pound professed cook. "Soups, *entrées*, jellies, ices."

Fluff had been read to sleep by an inoffensive Grimm's Goblin story, which had nothing either grim or goblinish about it; and Dora had returned to the drawing-room, where Stacie and Paul were sitting on each side of their mother's low easy-chair, and petting Spitz, upon whom they certainly lavished the greater part of their caresses. Spitz lay in his mistress's silken lap, and graciously submitted to be worshipped, giving a soft, hairy paw languidly to each of his adorers, with a condescending bend of his leg.

"We shall be away for nearly a month," said Mrs. Lerwick to her sister, "and I shall only stay for a night or two in Palatine Square when I come from the Continent, just to see about my winter frocks, and then go down to Dorsetshire. Your time will be finished here at the end of Stacie's holidays. I have written to Miss Warren, and she will be settled in her lodgings by the time the servants go to Heatherside, and ready to begin work with Paul."

Paul made a wry face. He was very proud of his book-learning; but he was not grateful to the lady who taught him.

"Are we to be at Heatherside alone, with only Miss Warren and Perry?" he asked, with a disgusted air.

He deferred so far to his aunt's opinion as to call his governess Miss Warren, but he could not bring himself to be equally polite in his mention of the nursery governess, whom everybody felt to be so very little above a nursemaid.

"She don't wear caps and aprons, and she don't look half as clean as the housemaids. That's the only difference," Paul had said, contemptuously, when the poor little governess was discussed.

"Can Aunt Dora stay at Heatherside till she's going to be married?" asked Paul.

"Your Aunt will be very busy. She will have her trousseau to think of."

"Why, she won't take a year to think about that," cried Stacie, contemptuously. "She don't bother her mind about frocks as you do, Mother. You will come to Heatherside, won't you, Auntie?"

Auntie replied with a hug, which Stacie accepted as Yes.

"Of course I shall be charmed for you to be there," said Mrs. Lerwick, "only I'm afraid you'll be awfully bored. As a rule, engaged girls find life a burden without their sweethearts."

"I don't think I should ever find life a burden with my nephews. And perhaps, when you and Tony are at Heatherside for the shooting, you'll let Mr. Doyle come to lunch or to tea now and then. He might happen to be stopping in the neighbourhood."

"No doubt he will happen to be wherever you are. Poor Dora! What fun you are with your first sweetheart! Yes, he shall come. Tony shall ask him with the shooters; and he shall stay as long as he likes. It shall not be a case of no followers allowed."

"No followers allowed," echoed Stacie. "That's what it ought to be. What does Auntie want with followers when she has us?"

There was a chorus of regrets among the Thomsons and Lerwicks at the Ramsgate station when the three boys and their aunt left for London. The Lerwicks would have liked to stay at Ramsgate all the year round. The Thomsons declared they hated the Isle of Thanet, and envied the Lerwicks for going to London, and then to Dorsetshire.

"London is the jolliest place in the world," protested the Thomson girls; "the shops are quite too lovely—and the theatres must be awfully nice."

"The theatres are all I care about in London," said one of the Thomson boys, who had been once in his life to Drury Lane in the pantomime season. "There's always something new coming out. When I'm reading for the Bar I shall be a regular first-nighter."

Stacie wanted to know what a first-nighter was, and Paul, who affected universal knowledge, would not allow Harry Thomson to explain, but cut in with a description of a smart audience at the Lyceum, taken straight from last week's *World*.

"Ah," said Stacie, "I shouldn't care a blow who was in the stalls if the piece was a good 'un, with Irving and Ellen Terry, or Toole and Eliza Johnstone acting in it. I shouldn't go to see the newspaper men and the professional beauties. They ain't in my line."

"Certainly not the newspaper men," sneered Paul, "for they have to be able to spell."

Aunt Dora went straight home to Mill Park to report herself to her father, and to refit for the autumn, and rejoined her nephews at Heatherside a fortnight after they left Ramsgate, in a neat little russet frock that repeated the colouring of the frost-touched beeches, and a neat little hat to match, with a grouse-claw mounted in silver which somebody had sent her from Scotland.

"Did Uncle Clem. send you that thing in your hat?" asked Fluff, with his accustomed pertness.

Dora's bright blush was a sufficient reply. And on being further questioned, she told her nephews that Clement Doyle was shooting in Argyllshire, and that he would not appear at Heatherside till the second week in October.

"Then he'll miss father's best shoot," said Paul, "for he's sure to have a lot of fellows here for the first."

There are halcyon days in every life, and that autumn season at Heatherside will always be remembered by Dorothea and her nephews, and by Ellinor Lerwick, as one of those bright and smiling intervals—a period in which all was pleasantness and peace—days of contentment undarkened by any dread of the future, spoilt by no idle yearnings for change or excitement.

Paul welcomed Miss Warren more amiably than usual, and attacked Todhunter and Virgil with equal gusto after his long fallow. He seemed, indeed, to relish his lessons as he had never relished them before.

"Ramsgate has done you good, young man," said the practical lady, when Paul had construed a page of the "Æneid" without a hitch. "Ozone is a capital thing for the intellect."

"Oh, I'm rather glad to get back to my work," answered Paul, carelessly. "I don't suppose young Billy Pitt ever had such a long holiday."

"Not he. They ground hard, and they caned hard under the Georges," said Miss Warren.

Paul had the early morning for a ramble or a ride, and the whole afternoon for his own amusement. Four hours' work between nine and one took him over a good deal of ground, Miss Warren devoting half that time to severe work—Latin, Greek, and mathematics—and the other half to what she called literature, which included modern languages—taught more out of books than out of dry-as-dust grammars—and history, studied in the newest and best writers—Green, Froude, Lecky, Stubbs, Freeman, and Gardiner. Paul was fond of history, and fond of literature in its best forms. He was not one of those boys who can read only boys' books. His imagination did not require to be for ever stimulated by stories of shipwreck and adventure, North American red-skins, or Polar bears. Scott's novels had been his favourite books ever since he could read; and in that world of romance he had found a golden gate to the world of reality. A boy who had read "Quentin Durward" was ready to be interested in King Louis of France and Duke Charles of Burgundy. A boy who had delighted in "Nigel" was eager to hear all that the historian could tell him about James the First and the England of Cecil and Bacon.

It was certainly a happy autumn. The two

boys were in high health after their Ramsgate holiday, and able to enjoy such rambles and excursions as they had never made before from Heatherside. Clement Doyle appeared upon the scene a month before Dora had expected him, and pilgrimages were arranged to all the interesting spots in the neighbourhood, pilgrimages in which even Mrs. Lerwick did not disdain to share when she returned from Marienbad, full of the condescension and charm of Royalties who had looked at her approvingly, or bought a painted paper-knife from her at a charity bazaar. Her husband was to arrive at Heatherside after the Doncaster meeting. They went to Corfe Castle and picnicked amidst the ruins one warm Wednesday, when hearts were beating high in the far-off throng, waiting for the result of the St. Leger. For that happy, innocent group—mother and aunt, children and governess—sitting in the shadow of those old towers which had reeled on their bases under Cromwell's artillery, that fair September afternoon was a time of peace and pleasantness ; but to some among the throng of loud-voiced humanity on the

Yorkshire flat this golden-hued autumn day was the day of doom.

Among the many who were heavily hit, Anthony Lerwick was not the lightest sufferer. That beautiful bay impostor, Badmash, had proved himself no more capable of winning the Leger than of winning the Derby, and his Doncaster performance had made a much worse show than his break-down at Epsom. Nor was Mr. Lerwick any luckier as a backer of other people's horses than he was in the more exalted character of owner. His losses on that Leger were heavy; but, of course, when a man does not know how rich he is, such losses count for very little. Yet for once in his life Mr. Lerwick was observed to take his punishment badly. He was depressed and out of sorts after the races, refused to dine with friends who were staying at the Reindeer Hotel, and hurried off to the train in what was considered a poor-spirited manner.

He was out of spirits when he came back to Heatherside, and took very little interest in the party which he himself had invited for the first;

although his keepers were jubilant at the prospects of the cover-shooting. Never had pheasants been more plentiful.

His friends came at the end of September, and stayed till the third week in October, and filled his house for him, and drank his champagne, and criticised his cook, and shot his birds; but this year he seemed to take less pleasure in their society than he had taken in the seasons that were gone. He looked ill, and he shot badly.

Clement Doyle saw that there was something amiss with his host; but he was not one of Tony Lerwick's intimates. He was not in touch with him. He only joined the shooters half a dozen times during his visit, not being as keen upon slaughtering pheasants as the men to whom big game and the hazards and adventures of the Indian jungle were unknown. He spent most of his days with Dorothea and her nephews. They played golf on the heath; they played pat-ball on the deserted lawn, where once there had been tennis tea-parties two or three times a week. The Caledonian game had put tennis out of fashion at Heatherside. He had engagements in the north, visits to friends and relatives which he would have to pay ; but he hung on, unwilling to leave his sweetheart even for a few weeks.

One day Mr. Lerwick's altered health made itself so obvious that even his wife's unobservant eyes discovered that something was wrong. He had no appetite ; he was nervous and dull. He allowed the family doctor to come and look at him, to satisfy his wife rather than from any faith he had in medicine ; but before the doctor saw the patient he was invited into the morning room, where he found Mrs. Lerwick sitting by the fire with Spitz, nursing her first winter cold.

"I am so frightfully susceptible to cold," she said, and the doctor was allowed to feel her pulse and hear all her troubles before he went to the smoking-room, where Mr. Lerwick was generally to be found on those rare occasions when he spent a morning indoors.

It was a dull, grey morning, and the wind and rain came every now and then in fierce gusts, rattling at the windows, and bending the deodaras in the shrubbery. It was weather that made even those perfect gardens unbeautiful; while the broad moorland in the distance was curtained in gloom, and the sea was the colour of lead.

"We ought all to get away from this horrid climate for the winter," Mrs. Lerwick said, shivering, and wrapping her china-crape shawl closer round her shoulders. "My husband has no chest. He is not fit to face an English winter. Don't you think now, Doctor, that the best thing we could do would be to pack our trunks and run away to the Riviera?"

Mrs. Lerwick had been impressed by this necessity within the last half-hour, during which she had been reading one of the society papers, in which everybody worth speaking about was reported as going, or intending to go, to the South.

November was a week old, and the world seemed to have turned suddenly to winter. Clement Doyle had gone back to his own people, to return to Heatherside for the Christmas holidays. The spacious villa, the large airy rooms, and wide corridors seemed almost empty without a house-party, and Ellinor Lerwick was feeling bored; and in that state of feeling the idea of finding another summer beside the Mediterranean came like a ray of light.

"I'm sure it would be the best thing for us to do," she repeated.

"It won't be the best thing for me, or for the people about here," answered the doctor, smiling at her child-like insistency. "I don't think there is much the matter with your lungs; but I'll go and look at Mr. Lerwick."

"Do; and pray overhaul him thoroughly. He is dreadfully narrow; but he will never acknowledge that he has a weak chest."

A footman conducted the doctor to the smoking-room, where Anthony Lerwick was sitting by the fire, half asleep.

Yes, he owned to having felt "under the weather" lately; but there was nothing amiss that he knew of. He allowed his chest to be sounded. It was certainly rather a narrow chest, though he was so tall and so well set-up.

"Mrs. Lerwick has been talking of the Riviera,"

said the doctor, "and I know she would like me to insist upon your going there. I can't quite conscientiously do that ; but it would do you no harm to escape an English winter. You are hot-house bred, both of you."

"You don't think I'm going into a consumption?"

"Not you, Mr. Lerwick. You have been taking rather too much out of yourself somehow, but your lungs are sound enough. It's your nerves that are out of order. For my own part, I should like to send you to St. Moritz."

"What, to shiver amidst everlasting snows? No, thank you."

"But as Mrs. Lerwick seems to have set her heart upon the Riviera——"

"Yes, yes. Nell must go where she likes. I'll take a villa at Monte Carlo. The air there is the finest along the coast."

Everything was settled within the next few days. An agent was communicated with, and the whole business was negotiated by telegraph. A villa was taken, the most exquisite of villas, a bijou, generally occupied by a Duchess, but which the Duchess did not happen to want this year. Mrs. Lerwick was delighted, and scanned the papers daily for announcements of the people who were going to Monte Carlo.

"We shall be rather early," she told Dora, "but all the world will be there in January. It will be better than a London season. There will be less of the small fry."

Paul and Fluff were to go with their father and mother; but Stacie's education was not to be interrupted. Mrs. Lerwick announced this decision with an air of supreme wisdom. He would finish his term at Elstree, and spend his holidays at Mill Park, where Dora would be delighted to have him.

Mr. and Mrs. Lerwick left Heatherside two days in advance of their sons. The boys were to travel with Dora and Miss Perry, the latter of whom was to leave them at Waterloo station in order to spend a couple of days with her people before starting for the Continent.

Poor little humdrum Miss Perry was vastly

elated at the idea of being taken to that enchanted city of which she had read so much, even though she was to be a genteel drudge there, doing a nursemaid's work in attendance upon Fritz; for it had been decided that Pittman's services were no longer required, and the austere female had left Heatherside with a month's wages and a handsome present, and a reserved force of indignation swelling her matronly bosom.

She prophesied an early grave for Fritz, in her parting conversation with the housekeeper.

" I give that poor child six months at the most, with that empty-headed girl to look after him—or to make believe to look after him—for that's about all it will be," she said, shaking her head dolorously, just before stepping into the station brougham.

Paul and Fritz liked the idea of a foreign country, a place where there was pigeon-shooting, and where it was always summer. But they grieved a little at parting with Aunt Dora.

" It seems hard lines for you after you've put off your marriage on purpose to be with us," Paul said;

but Dora protested that she would in no case have cared to be married before June.

"We shall be back in March, mother says, and then you must stay with us in the Square, and buy your trousseau," said Paul, and the arrangement seemed alike natural and convenient.

"I wish you were coming with us, little Auntie. Mother ought to take you," said Fluff. "She didn't want to take Pincher, only I made her. I said I wouldn't go without Pincher. She would have taken Spitz, and left Pincher. I do call that selfishness. As if my dog wasn't ever so much more to me than her dog is to her. Why, he sleeps *in* my bed; and she won't have Spitz even outside hers; because of her satin counterpane, I suppose," concluded Fluff, contemptuously, drawing upon himself serious reproof for undutiful speech about his mother.

CHAPTER XIV.

IN DEEP WATERS.

THE journey from Heatherside to London was almost too short for the boys, as it allowed no halting-places for the purchase of buns and chocolate. The Bournemouth express only stopped at Brockenhurst and at Southampton, where no inviting edibles were brought to the carriage window.

"I call this a beastly train," said Fluff, sprawling in all the luxury of the Pullman, kicking his restless legs upon the broad velvet cushions, and looking listlessly at the passing landscape, after having exhausted a large supply of pictorial papers.

The carriage was waiting for them at Waterloo, where they left poor little Perry tripping off with a porter to find an omnibus that would carry her and her small Gladstone to the wilds of South London. A footman was in attendance on Miss Hampden and her nephews, and he was to collect the luggage and take it to Palatine Square in a station omnibus. There was nothing to detain Dora and her charges. They squeezed themselves into the miniature brougham, and the high-stepping horse trotted off with them, with his head in the air, scorning the shabbiness of the York-road.

There was no servant on the box, and Dora and the boys had to let themselves out of the carriage and ring the bell. Fluff rang with all his might, holding Pincher by his chain, while Paul performed a spirited solo on the knocker.

The door was opened by a housemaid—a fact almost without precedent in the history of Palatine Square. In the long blank spaces of the family's absence this vision of a woman in an apron opening one half of the massive double door might be common enough; since at those periods the house was given over to desolation and three servants on board wages. But that a housemaid should appear in the entrance hall to-day—when mother, with all her paraphernalia of luxury and splendour, was on the premises—was a thing to make Paul wonder, and to draw words of mockery from the livelier Fluff.

"Where's your powder, Sarah, and why haven't you got on your silk stockings?" asked Fluff, entering the house in an involuntary run, dragged by the muscular and excited Pincher, who rushed in as if the hall were a rat-warren.

Sarah took no notice of Fluff's lively address, although she was fond of him, and considered him a wit. She turned with a pale, distressed face to Miss Hampden.

"Oh, ma'am, we're in such trouble!" she murmured faintly.

Dora was quick to take fright. That look seemed to turn her blood to ice.

"What's the matter? Is your mistress ill?"

"Oh, the poor missus! It's worst for her. It was only ten minutes ago. And there's a p'liceman up there—a-frightening of poor missus. As if it wasn't bad enough without a p'liceman!"

Paul and his aunt heard this awful speech, and

looked at each other aghast. Fluff had followed Pincher into the inner hall, and was out of hearing. The noise of the terrier's chain, and the patter of his claws on the marble, drowned Sarah's muffled accents.

Suddenly there came a chilling sound from the landing above—the spacious landing where Mrs. Lerwick used to stand for hours, smiling down at the procession of beautiful women and beautiful gowns, at the men, who all looked exactly alike except those who wore stars and ribands, whom Fluff and Paul admired immensely, or the ecclesiastics, with handsome black silk legs, and a grave dignity which impressed Fluff almost as much as the jewelled orders.

It was the sound of a dog's piteous whining, the sad imploring whimper which Paul had heard so often when the pampered favourite was shut out of Mrs. Lerwick's rooms. While they looked up and listened, the whimper changed to a long-drawn dolorous howl, a sound so unmatched in melancholy that it has been taken by the popular mind to be a thing of evil omen, prophetic of death.

Dora rushed upstairs, followed closely by Paul;
but on the half-flight she stopped, and seized the
boy's hand convulsively.

"Go back, dear," she entreated. "Go back to
Fluff, and take him into the dining-room. If there
is any accident—anything dreadful—he had better
not know."

"Auntie, I can't! I must know."

The words were spoken on both sides with
breathless rapidity; and then aunt and nephew
hurried on. There was a resolute intensity in
Paul's countenance which made him look like a
man, with all a man's sternness of purpose. He
grasped Dora's wrist with his bare hand, and she
felt the coldness of his touch even through her
glove.

Yes, there was a policeman on the landing. He
stood at ease looking out of the window into the
emptiness of the wintry square, and seemed to
have no business there except to contemplate
Nature as illustrated by the smoke-blackened
branches of London elms and sycamores. He
himself looked harmless enough; but the presence

of that blue coat and severe helmet was frightening. Something had happened, Paul knew; but what? He thought of his mother—a carriage accident—a mad dog—a gown that had caught fire—of his father—thought helplessly, seeming in a few moments to explore vast wildernesses of horror.

Mr. Lerwick's room was at the end of a short passage on the half-flight. It was at that door Spitz lay whining. It was there he lifted up his head and repeated that prolonged lamentation which had struck terror to Paul's heart in the hall below.

Paul ran along the passage, followed by Dora. He tried to open the door, while the little silken-haired dog sniffed his clothes, and leapt up at him, licking his left hand impetuously as it hung loose by his side. The door was locked.

"Father, father, let me in, please!" implored Paul.

There was no answer, and he knocked, and again entreated: "Father! Somebody! What has happened? Let me in—it's Paul!" and he knocked louder and louder, with a hand that shook like a leaf.

It seemed a long time to Dora Hampden, standing close behind him with one arm wound about him, as if by the passion of her love she could shield him from that unknown horror behind the locked door. That a tragedy had happened, that horror of some kind was waiting for them, she knew too well. She could hear the subdued murmurs of several voices inside the spacious room, and the sound of a woman's hysterical sobs; and below, on the marble pavement of the hall, she could hear the scampering of Pincher's feet, and Fluff's silver-clear voice talking to him.

Presently the door opened, and a stranger came out, shutting it so quickly behind him that neither of those who waited without could look into the room. They heard the key turned in the lock. The stranger was a grave-looking, middle-aged man, with a greyish beard and spectacles, and carried his hat in his hand. A doctor, evidently. Neither Dora nor Paul had any need to wonder about him.

"Is this Master Lerwick?" he asked, laying his hand on Paul's shoulder.

"Yes, and I am his mother's sister," answered Dora. "For pity's sake tell us what has happened. Can't I see my sister? I thought I heard her crying in that room."

"You shall see her presently. She is being looked after. Could I speak to you alone—anywhere?"

"No, no, no," Paul cried, passionately. "You are to tell me as well as Aunt. It's my mother that's crying—it's my father that's dead."

The doctor started and looked at him, dumb-founded.

"I know he is dead," said Paul, looking at the doctor.

"He is very—seriously—ill."

"He is dead!" cried Paul. "Do you think I'm a baby? Let me go to him! Let me go to my mother! Why did they lock the door? I won't have it. I will go—I will see him."

He pushed past the stranger with a determination which startled the man of wide experience, and ran at the door and battered it with his fists.

"Mother, mother, let me in. It is I—Paul. I will see him!"

Again the key turned in the lock, and his mother came out, with disordered hair and streaming eyes. She came out of a crowd, as it seemed to Paul, in his momentary glimpse of the space behind her, a crowd of scared faces and murmuring tongues; then the door closed again, and again the key was turned in the lock. There were two doors, with a three-foot passage between them, and he heard the inner door close, and then the murmuring voices were still, and he and his mother were standing face to face.

She clung to him and kissed him, distractedly, and then, looking over his head at Dora, she asked: "Does Fluff know?"

Her darling's voice answered her question, ringing out from the hall below in gay laughter.

"O God, it's too dreadful!" she muttered, with white lips. "He was talking to me less than an hour ago; and now—— "

She stopped, choked by her sobs. Paul put his arm round her; and the doctor touched her gently

on the shoulder, begging her to compose herself,
to remember her children, and to bear in mind
that their father's sudden death must not be made
to seem more awful than death—sudden death,
especially—must always be.

He spoke in a very low voice, slowly and im-
pressively; and there was a meaning in his voice
which Dora seemed shudderingly to understand.
There was something exceptionally terrible in this
sudden death, she thought; something that the
dead man's children must never know.

"Go upstairs with your son, dear lady," said the
doctor. "I'll bring you the little boy."

"Yes, bring him to me—my Fritz, my idol—all
I have to live for in the world now," sobbed Mrs.
Lerwick, as she went totteringly upstairs, clinging
mechanically to Paul, her wild eyes staring straight
before her, all the delicate prettiness vanished out
of her tear-stained face and tumbled gown, with
its fragile lace trimmings hanging in rags about
her neck and arms. She looked as if she had
been crawling on the ground—as if she had been
beating her head against the wall. Despair had

altered her from head to foot. It had changed
her into another woman; and yet the innate
weakness and shallowness of her character were
as marked in her day of sorrow as ever they had
been in her days of joy.

Dora went upstairs with her sister, and made
her sit on the sofa by the fire, while Paul sat
quietly beside her, holding her hand, and knowing
that she cared very little about him, that she was
hardly conscious of his presence. Yet when Fluff
appeared the floodgates of her tears would be
loosened again; and she would melt in a passion
of love for the child she had chosen; the one
chosen out of three; the other two being almost
as strangers.

Spitz had followed them up to his accustomed
apartment, and had coiled himself in a circle
close against the marble fender, rejoicing in the
warmth, and perhaps forgetting the tragic mystery
that had come with a sudden fear and trembling
into the dimness of his canine intellect.

"Mother," Paul asked, quietly, "when did father
die?"

"Not half an hour ago. Oh, Paul, I feel as if it were long ages ago—I hardly know what the world was like before," sobbed his mother. "It seems to have been always so—always this misery."

"But God will have pity upon us all," murmured Dora, kneeling by the sofa, with her head leaning against Paul's shoulder, praying for him and for his mother; praying dumbly in every interval of silence. "We must love each other all the more dearly," she went on. "We must try to be all the world to each other. You and I, Nell, and the three dear boys."

"You are going away next year," said Paul, bitterly. "You'll soon be out of it."

"I won't leave you till you're happy again, Paul," she answered softly.

"Then you'll never go; for that will never be," answered Paul; and then he spoke to his mother again, with a grave resolution that seemed to exercise a kind of authority over her weakness— a child of twelve being so much her intellectual superior. "What was the matter? Why did father die?"

"He fell down dead," she faltered, and then muttered inarticulate syllables, with white lips, and then looked helplessly at her sister. " I think the doctor said it was heart disease."

"Poor father! Dead! And he was always kind to us—he was never angry—he was always generous!"

"Too generous!" sobbed his mother. "He threw his money out of the windows. He gave it to everybody who asked him. Oh! no, no, no, Dora!" as if answering a mute reproach in her sister's face. "I am not blaming the dead. He was very good to me—he spoilt me—as if I had been a foolish child. But to think of all the money we have wasted — and now we are paupers!"

"Mother!"

"Yes, Paul, we are beggars. There will be no Elstree for you, no Harrow, no Oxford for Stacie. You will have to go to Australia and make roads for your daily bread. There will be nothing for Fluff—nothing. We may have to starve, perhaps."

The doctor opened the door gently, and Fluff,

still dragging, or dragged by, Pincher, ran into the room, and flung himself sobbing into his mother's lap. She clasped him to her breast, and cried over him and kissed his soft flaxen hair with her parched lips, and held him strained to her heart.

"Oh, mother! mother! mother!" he sobbed helplessly.

The strange doctor had told him vaguely that there was trouble in the house. His father was ill. He would have to comfort his mother. Her sons must love her with all the strength of their hearts in her day of sorrow. This was what the unknown doctor had told Fluff; and the child felt that all the house was full of fear and trouble, and that misery too great for words had fallen upon him and his brothers.

CHAPTER XV.

WITHOUT RUDDER OR COMPASS.

ANTHONY LERWICK had died by his own hand. That was the secret which Paul had guessed, in spite of the doctor's veiled words, of the dumbness of the servants, who, albeit they were never tired of talking over the tragedy below-stairs, were careful to give no hint of the dreadful truth to the dead man's children.

Neither Eustace nor Fritz knew the true story of their father's death. They believed what they were told, and they were told only that he had died with terrible suddenness—had dropped down dead in his own room at the back of the house, half an hour after leaving his wife's morning room. Eustace, summoned from Elstree on the day after his father's death, was quite as easily satisfied as

Fluff had been, quite as willing to accept his aunt's version of the sorrowful story.

"And now that God has taken away your father, you must love your poor mother more than ever, Stacie," said Dora, in her low, pleading voice, as she sat over the fire in the schoolroom, with Stacie and Paul, while Fluff and the dogs were below in his mother's room. Mrs. Lerwick would not have her youngest child out of her sight for an hour; but it seemed as if she could hardly endure the presence of the other two.

"There are so many of you," she complained piteously. "You bewilder me. You make my head ache, worse than it has been aching ever since——"

Ever since the sharp report of a pistol had startled her from her idle dream of life—that ringing sound which had brought the servants hurrying into the hall—the scared faces gathering on the stairs—the silly French maid putting her head out of the first available window to shriek into the square, with a shrill scream that attracted a passing policeman, and brought him into the house, to establish the fact that the master had shot himself, and to give speedy information to the Coroner.

When a gentleman dies by his own hand in such a place as Palatine Square, the melancholy consequences of his death are lightened as much as they can be by the respectful behaviour of officials. Mr. Lerwick's tragic fate was known to very few people before the appearance of a paragraph under the heading of "Inquests," which told how Mr. Anthony Lerwick, of Palatine Square, had committed suicide in a fit of temporary insanity.

His sons were not allowed to see that paragraph. All newspapers were kept from them by Dora's watchful care; and in the first week or two of mourning Stacie was indifferent even to the result of half a dozen football matches, and content to exist without any news of the outer world.

It was only Paul whose shrewd eyes had pierced the dark veil that hung over the day of his home-coming; and he breathed no word of his suspicion to either of his brothers. There was deepest shame to him in the thought that his father had so died;

for Miss Warren had taught him to think that what was courage in a Roman was cowardice in a Christian.

"A Christian's ruling thought is duty," she had said to him once when they had been reading of Seneca's death, "and no Christian would wish to leave this life while there was anybody in the world who wanted him, or any good deed that he could do."

"There were Christians who lived in caves," Paul had replied, "who never did any good to anybody, and who didn't even wash themselves."

"They were blind followers of blind leaders, Paul. They had strayed very far from the light of the Gospel."

"Poor old beggars! They had a bad time of it," commented the boy, who had just been reading an English version of "Homo Sum."

He had read *Hamlet* with his governess, who was an ardent Shakespearean, and they had discussed the catastrophe, and the Prince's passionate appeal to Horatio, urging him to endure the burden of life a little longer in order that he might tell the world the truth about his murdered master.

"Horatio had a duty to do, you see, Paul," moralized Miss Warren, "and it would have been base in him to throw away his life because he had done with happiness."

The boy's thinking powers had been developed in many an argument with his serious middle-aged governess, who had taught him to care for books which few boys of his age can relish. The absorbing interests of cricket, the ardent pleasures of Rugger or Socker had been kept out of his life. The doctors had pronounced him too delicate to begin his athletic education yet awhile; except in the gentlest form of Swedish gymnastics, or such mild cricket or pat-ball as could be played in a garden of girls. So educated, Paul had developed into a thinking machine; and it was quite as difficult for him to desist from thinking as it was for Stacie and Fluff to think.

He brooded over his father's fate with deepest melancholy. It was his first experience of sorrow —the first dark cloud of trouble that had closed around his life; and it seemed to him that no gleam of sun could ever penetrate that utter blackness of grief and shame. Yes, there was shame mingled with his sorrow for the good-tempered, easy-going, open-handed father, of whose life, and thoughts, and feelings he had known so little. He was ashamed that his father should have been so wanting in Christian faith and heroic endurance that he should not have been able to look ruin calmly in the face. For, after all, what could it matter to a man whether he lived at Palatine Square or in a labourer's cottage? He thought of Cincinnatus; of all those shining lights he had read about with Miss Warren. He thought of the Iron Duke and his narrow bed and hard pillow, of his Spartan habits, and luxury of benevolence. His father had fled from the evil to come—only that evil of narrow means which braver spirits meet so bravely—and had left wife and sons to face the trouble he thought intolerable. It was a terrible thing to think of that kindly man, whose pleasant smile had been so marked a characteristic of the young, bright face that Paul could hardly recall his features without the aid of a photograph. The smile, the cheerful voice, the well-set-up figure had been the man.

"Poor father!" mused Paul. " If he had stopped to think about us all, and what he would make us suffer by such a death, he would never have done it. He was much too kind."

The shame was even worse than the grief in Paul's mind. He thought that his mother and her sons would be always spoken of with a kind of scornful pity, as the widow and children of a suicide. And Paul had a stubborn pride which revolted against the idea of pity. He brooded over his trouble all day; he dreamt of hideous things at night; but he never hinted at his suspicions, even to his Aunt Dora. Still less would he have stooped to ask a question of a servant. He hoped that no one would ever speak to him of the tragedy; but sometimes in those dismal winter days, which closed in darkness long before tea-time, he felt that it would have been a comfort to spend an hour with Miss Warren, talking with her, not of his own grief, but of trouble in general; of the great burden of trouble which the world was bearing, while people in Palatine Square were giving big evening parties, and spending three or four hundred pounds upon the floral decorations for a single night—flowers that were faded before morning, mere rubbish to be stripped off the walls and swept away.

Remembering how the large lofty rooms—the stately staircase—had been transformed into a garden of roses for his mother's last ball, he could not but think of the money that had been spent in that house, and how few traces of it were left. All that had been spent and achieved there seemed but a vision of splendour, seen for a moment amidst the changing images of a dream.

Poor, helpless, feather-headed mother, who was moping through the wintry days, sitting over the fire, amidst the expensive litter of her morning room, in the gaudy *deshabille* of a scarlet and gold Japanese tea-gown, while huge *cartons* from the mourning warehouse were stacked in her bedroom, waiting till she had courage to put on widow's weeds.

Cards and letters of condolence had flowed in upon her, mingled with circulars from stone-masons, eager to be at work upon marble or granite, in honour of the dead man. The hall and staircase were still pervaded by faint odours of lilies and tube-roses, which had been heaped upon the coffin; and going up and down stairs, Paul sometimes trod upon a tube-rose or a gardenia that had snapped off at the stem, or a withered spray of maiden-hair fern.

He remembered how that spacious staircase, and the closed door of his father's sitting-room, had oppressed his spirits last June in the silence of the summer twilight and the great empty house, and how a nameless horror had scared him as he passed those tenantless rooms. Another boy might have told himself that those melancholy sensations were a supernatural portent; but Miss Warren had taught Paul to clear his mind of superstition, and he knew that his feelings had meant no more than the natural sadness of solitude and summer evening.

But henceforward that passage leading to his

father's room—the recessed window yonder, where the policeman had stood like a wooden figure, taking no part in the tragedy—would be haunted with ghastly memories. He longed to escape from the gloomy splendour, from a house which he had never loved. He felt that he should hardly care if they had to move into two or three garrets in a London alley: rooms as wretched as that garret in a court out of Holborn where Chatterton, the poet, once lay dead. He could hardly understand his mother's wailing about departure from Palatine Square, as a calamity not to be thought of without hysteria.

"We shall have to give up everything, Paul—everything!" she cried, in one of those brief interviews which she accorded to her elder sons, while Fluff, who spent most of his time in her room, sprawled on the hearthrug, teasing Spitz. "The horrid creditors will take everything—all my silver things—all the ornaments in this room —because, though they are my very own, and I bought them, they are to count as furniture, Dora says."

Miss Hampden had been the only person to see the lawyers who had charge of her sister's interests, and who came between Anthony Lerwick's widow and the troops of commercial wolves who bore down upon the house in Palatine Square—tradesmen of every kind, from the coach-builders who built Mr. Lerwick's drag and Mrs. Lerwick's victoria, to the cobbler who mended the stablemen's shoes. Most of these traders had received hundreds, and many of them thousands, from the house in Palatine Square; but all had money owing to them, much or little, when the famous firm of Lerwick and Lerwick stopped suddenly one morning, like a watch whose mainspring was broken.

Sudden as the stoppage was, it had not come without warning. Anthony Lerwick had been told quite enough by accountants, managers, head clerks, and other sage advisers, to know that all was not as it once had been with the house of Lerwick. The great flood-tide of prosperity had gone down. The river of gold was running low and sluggishly. They were passing through a crisis, his manager told him. The net results of the year's trading were far from satisfactory, wrote the accountants, in a letter to Anthony himself, labelled " Private."

Mr. Lerwick thought the accountants had taken an unwarrantable liberty in so writing to him; and he had thought hardly any more about it. He had heard of that "crisis" before, and of net results that were unsatisfactory. The phrases were to his mind mere forms of speech, which only meant that no business could make the same profits every year.

Then the manager, who was also a junior partner, had appeared early one morning in Palatine Square, with a proposal that Lerwick and Lerwick should be turned into a limited company, capital two millions. It was a Goodwood morning, and the brougham was at the door to take Mr. and Mrs. Lerwick to the station. The manager showed his principal a type-written draft of the prospectus he proposed issuing. The firm was solvent. The firm had been making large profits within the last ten years. A very good

R

account—a judicious account—could be given of the last three years' trading, though, by comparison with an earlier period, it was not assuring. The manager saw powerful rivals in the future, firms that had grown to unexpected magnitude out of small beginnings, and he feared Lerwick and Lerwick would never be as they had been. Now was the time to invite the public to come in. Later any such invitation might be ineffectual. Mr. Lerwick pretended to listen, with his eye on the railway time-table, glanced over the prospectus with a casual air, and said he was quite willing to make the business into a company, and to wash his hands of all trouble—"as if he had ever taken any!" thought the manager—provided he got as good an income as he was getting now.

The manager hummed and hesitated.

"There would be a lump sum to come to you out of the capital, but you'd have to take at least half your money in shares. Of course you have not been living up to your income since you came of age."

"Of course I have, my dear fellow. What's a

man's income meant for except to keep him and his belongings? Besides, I've been deuced unlucky with my stable."

"My dear Lerwick," the manager began, gravely, trying to buttonhole him, "if I were you, I'd retrench—I would indeed. I'd cut things as close as possible. The iron trade is not what it was."

"I heard that when I was at Eton," said Lerwick; "and I heard it again at Brasenose, when the governor objected to my skewbald team. I don't want to hear it from you, chappie. Nothing is what it once was. The English race-horse ain't what he was when Voltigeur was foaled. He's a delusion and a snare. Ta-ta. I mustn't lose the Goodwood express. Do as you please about the prospectus."

In the ears of most men, such an interview would have sounded like the funeral knell of fortune; but it hardly discomposed Anthony Lerwick. He had heard of other great firms being made into limited liability companies, and he looked upon the thing as a fashion of the day. He did not care what form his income assumed, so long as he had plenty of money to spend, and was able to fling a cheque on account to any tradesman who pestered him for money, without troubling himself to look at his bill.

"I mean to go into your account some day, Joskins," he said to his coachbuilder, "when I have an hour's leisure."

The idler a man's life is, the less leisure there is in it, as a rule. Mr. Lerwick had been in a hurry ever since he left Eton; hurrying from the river to the race-course; from the tennis-court to the golf-ground; from Hurlingham to Ascot. He had been hurried along a stream of pleasures, and had never had time to think. And then one morning—that cruel morning when he and his wife had been talking of the delicious change from London fogs and the creeping cold of an English November to the bright blue sky and the bright blue sea, and the orange garden and roses round their villa at Monte Carlo,—in the midst of their Fool's Paradise, the blow had fallen upon him,—a long grave letter from the junior partner telling him how every effort to transform Lerwick and Lerwick into a company had failed, and how the business was hopelessly insolvent.

He was beggared—he and his wife and his children. He was alone when the letter was handed him, and he read it quietly through, every word sinking into his heart with a physical pain, as if it were a bit of lead. Bankruptcies and failures in South America, in the West Indies, at the Cape, had come crashing down, blow after blow, upon Lerwick and Lerwick, until the central house lay crushed and annihilated, a heap of ashes, out of which not a grain of gold would ever be squeezed again.

"I tried to tell you the plain truth that day I took you the prospectus," wrote the manager; "but I was hopeful then that we should weather the storm and get a new start. I did not know that the end was so near."

The end! Anthony Lerwick took his pass-book out of a drawer in his desk, and looked at his banking account, made up a few days before.

There had been seven hundred and sixty-three pounds to his credit when the account was balanced; and he knew that, over and above innumerable house accounts, milliners, tailors, jewellers, decorators, and florists, he owed at least three thousand for his losses at the Doncaster meeting — money which he must pay, or face instant disgrace.

He looked round him wildly, like an animal at bay, and clapped his hand to his forehead with a desperate movement.

To face the world a pauper—he who had always been rich! Impossible! He pulled open another drawer hurriedly, with a hand that shook like a leaf. It was the drawer in which he kept the revolver he used for practice in a shooting-gallery. Three minutes after, the report of a pistol rang through the house, and brought Ellinor Lerwick rushing from her room on the floor above, awakened in that one awful moment from her dream of life.

CHAPTER XVI.

KISSING THE ROD.

THERE were now only one managing mind and one busy pen in Palatine Square, and the pen and the mind belonged to Dora Hampden. The little Auntie had the whole burden of those broken lives laid upon her shoulders. Her father wrote briefly, "I am very sorry for poor Nell and her boys. You had better bring them all to Mill Park as soon as they are ready to move. Give my love to Nell, and tell her not to fret."

And having written thus, Mr. Hampden thought he had done his duty as a father, and that he was free to hunt three days a week, and drink his half-bottle of port every evening after dinner, in his accustomed self-indulgent placidity. He was not the man to make himself more unhappy than the occasion demanded.

The little Auntie wrote her sister's letters, held daily communication with the lawyers, and paid off and dismissed all the servants who could possibly be dispensed with ; and thus in a single day that stately household dwindled to an elderly couple who were to be caretakers till the "mansion" passed into other hands, and the good-natured Sarah, who protested she wouldn't mind how she slaved for her "poor missus and them dear boys."

It was the little Auntie who husbanded the small stock of ready money which the lawyers gave her to pay the servants and carry on the diminished housekeeping ; for those fashionable tradesmen who had sent the very best and choicest of their goods to the house in Palatine Square, fawning on the housekeeper, flattering the butler, and cajoling the cook, were now indisposed to give any further credit for so much as a quartern loaf.

In spite of the princely income that he had dispensed ever since he came of age, Anthony Lerwick had wound up his life deeply in debt. He had paid vast sums, and he owed vast sums. Those handsome cheques which he had flung right and left, with casual munificence, had only served to keep his purveyors in good humour. And now the bills poured in, and the tradespeople were clamorous ; for it was whispered everywhere that Mr. Lerwick had died insolvent; and those who had profited by his extravagance were loud in denouncing his folly.

To take her sister and the boys away from all this degradation and misery was Dora's earnest endeavour. They were not to go back to Heatherside. The Dorsetshire villa, the building of which had cost a small fortune, was to be sold, with all its expensive contents, save those things which could be claimed as the widow's personal belongings. They were never more to play tennis on the lovely lawn above the sea ; never again to look from the familiar windows at the picturesque chines and bays of the Dorsetshire coast—Swanage and Lulworth, and away to the Bill of Portland. Country house and town house were to vanish from them in the same dark cloud. A lion had come out of the wood to devour them, and the lion's name was Debt.

Paul, who did all the thinking for the three, could not help remembering all he had heard about the prices paid for his mother's frocks, and the money his father had lost at every big race-meeting. People had talked before him as if he had neither ears to hear nor a mind to remember; and the knowledge he had gained in this way smote him hard at this time of trouble. He could not but remember all that idle talk of dress and dressmakers, as he sat moodily by the fire in his mother's bedroom, while his aunt turned over the piles of finery—now such useless finery—and sorted the things that were to be sold, or given away to poor relations, and the things that were to be kept. Oh, those pearl fringes, those ostrich-feather trimmings, jewelled embroideries, spider-web laces, satins, gauzes, muslins! His heart sickened at the sight of them.

"Why do women dress like that?" he asked, pointing contemptuously to the mountain of perishable splendour. "Why can't a woman wear a black velvet gown, with a bit of point lace on her neck every night, as a man wears his dress suit?"

"An evening party would look very dismal, Paul, if all the women were in black velvet," Dora answered, gently, looking up from the weary toil of folding and arranging, and stooping over trunks and imperials.

All the packing had fallen to her share. Her sister was fit for nothing, and attempted nothing.

"You might as well say men look dismal. But women might wear coloured velvets and silks and handsome things, without all that trumpery— feathers and beads and bits of glass sewn on to lace—rags and tatters. An Indian squaw may care for such things, because she knows no better; but for a sensible woman to squander hundreds and thousands——"

"Paul, it's very unkind of you to talk like that now, when your poor mother is so unhappy."

"Oh, I don't mean any unkindness about mother. She's no worse than all the other women. They wear what the dressmakers tell them to wear. I've heard mother's Frenchwoman preaching to her. She was to wear this, or that —no, not beads, this year, nothing but feathers.

Not lace, but only jewelled gauze. It used to make me sick. Mother seemed to have no will or opinion of her own."

"I suppose it is good for trade," sighed Dora.

"I dare say it's good for half a dozen trades-people; but Sarah says the women who sew on the beads and make the feather trimmings are almost starving in their garrets. I hope you won't have any beads and feathers in your trousseau, little Auntie."

"Not many, Paul; but I am not going to think of my trousseau yet awhile."

She gave a little sigh as she said this, and a tear or two dropped into the box over which she was bending. The aspect of her life was changed by her brother-in-law's death. Her sister's help-lessness frightened her; for it made her think that the fortunes of the three boys would have to depend mostly upon her. She knew how much and how little their grandfather would do for them. He would let them eat at his table, and sleep under his roof; but he would not think and strive and plan for their future. He would consider that he did enough for them if he were kind to them in the present. It was not in his nature to take much trouble.

Some one would have to take trouble; some one would have to think and strive; so that these three boys might be educated and trained to be busy bread-winning men; so that they might suffice for themselves, and be a help and comfort to their helpless mother. Dora, even in her rural experience, had heard enough about the struggle for life to know that it would be no easy task to fit her nephews for gentleman-like employments, and to obtain such employment for them when they should be old enough to work. Friends would have to be entreated; interest would have to be invoked; every name in her father's address-book would have to be studied, in the search for friends who might help.

Sisyphus had to roll one stone up a hill; but here was little Dora Hampden who had to roll three stones up the cruel steep that leads to the Temple of Fortune. That was to be her sole business in life—that, and not her own happiness.

They depended upon her, poor little lads; and she loved them, and would count no sacrifice too great to be made for their welfare.

Her sweetheart had been in Palatine Square for an hour or two on the day of the funeral, and had comforted her, and offered to do anything in the world that could be helpful to the mourners. And since that day he had been in the north, visiting his people, and he was to return to town to-day, and was coming to see her in the late afternoon. This afternoon's interview was to be of some importance in their lives; and it was the thought of what she had to say to her lover that brought those tears to Dora Hampden's eyes.

When four o'clock struck they were together in one of the desolate drawing-rooms, where the foggy evening outside was hardly brightened by the pinched little fire in the brass grate, and the one lamp which Sarah had considered sufficient for the occasion. Everything in the shape of ornament had been removed; and the chairs and sofas wore the holland coverings that had been put on them when the family were on the eve of departure.   The shabbiest parlour in Brixton or Camberwell would have been less depressing of aspect than those spacious and lofty rooms which were soon to figure in a house-agent's catalogue.

"My dearest, how glad you will be to get away from this ghastly house," said Clement Doyle. "My heart aches to think of the fortnight you have spent here—while I have been going about among pleasant places and people."

"Yes, I shall be very glad to leave.   The house seems haunted to all of us.   The poor boys are miserable—and Ellinor—well, her state is quite hopeless here—but I think she will be better when I get her home.   I finished the packing an hour ago ; and we shall be quite ready to start by the express to-morrow morning."

"And I shall be ready to take care of you all—and of your luggage—and your dogs.   The dogs are to go with you, of course ?"

"Yes, indeed.   We could hardly live without the dogs.   Pincher has been the only ray of sunshine in these dreary days.   He made the boys take him to the Green Park every morning, and but for him, I don't believe they would have left the house."

"Well, we must try and make them happy in Devonshire. I shall establish myself at Bideford for the winter—and perhaps in the spring I might set up a bit of a yacht at Clovelly, and we could have excursions——"

"Oh, Clement, the boys will have to be at school. I have been finding out all about schools; and I think Helstone will be best. Nell and I can have a nice house there, and a garden, for less money than almost anywhere. And she will be far away from all the fine people she knew in London. I hope there will be something left— some little income—when this house and all the expensive furniture, and Heatherside, and her jewels, have been sold, and all the creditors paid."

"God knows! He seems to have left a mass of indebtedness. To spend so much in so few years, and yet to owe so much! It is a financial problem."

" Father must help her."

" He will help her, no doubt. And we can help her, Dora. We shall be able to spare her at least a hundred a year—and in the wilds of Cornwall that will buy a good many breakfasts and dinners."

" You help her!" cried Dora, with a shocked look. "You toil in India for my sister and her children. No, no! That would be too unfair."

" Unfair to help my wife's sister! And as to toil, the work I do yonder is work I love. And it is a good thing for a man in India not to have too much cash. It may mean a Polo pony or two less in the year. That's all."

Dora's cheeks glowed and her eyes shone as she looked at him.

"No wonder I love you," she murmured, with her hands clasped in his; "how noble you are! how generous!"

"Because I am willing to help my belongings— verily a tremendous hero. Have you any idea how many fellows in the East are toiling for those they love in the West; for mothers and sisters, and young brothers, and maiden aunts? My dearest, it won't give me the least trouble to

S

contribute my poor little hundred.   Part of my income comes to me from England, so there'll be no loss by exchange.   I shall just tell my agent here to send your sister a quarterly cheque."

" Nell would never accept your bounty."

"Don't call it by such an ugly name.   Of course she will accept.   Widows and orphans— the wounded in the battle of life—are a charge upon able-bodied soldiers.   They have to be cared for.   And your three boys are going to grow up into three money-earning men.   That fellow Paul ought to be a judge of the Supreme Court before he's fifty—and the eldest would make a very good forester.   We'll send him to Cooper's Hill.   Fluff, the spoilt one, shall go to sea.   They'll comb him down on board the *Britannia*.   There'll be plenty of time for us to arrange and settle things before July."

" Before July !   Oh ! Clement, that is what I have been wanting to say to you.   Our marriage must be put off—for three or four years—till your next long leave,.if—if you care to wait for me."

" I don't care to wait—I won't wait !   There is no reason."

"There is, dear; an unanswerable reason. I can't leave those boys in their mother's care—for three or four years to come."

"Not in their mother's care? Who can be so fit to take care of them as their mother? What can you do for them that she cannot do?"

"Ah, you don't know, Clement—you don't know how helpless she is."

"She must learn to be helpful. It is her business in life to care for her children," Doyle answered sternly. "If she is a good woman she will very soon learn to do her duty."

"But not in a few months, Clement. There will be so little time for learning between now and July. She has broken down completely. Think of what she has suffered. She saw him— she was the first to go to him—saw him lying dead at her feet—and he had left her half an hour before in health and high spirits—and all the world was bright with them, as she thought, poor thing. And in a moment she knew that he was dead—and all was changed."

She burst into tears, and her sweetheart com-

forted her with all those tender words which
lovers find in hours of sorrow.

"My dear love, we are not going to abandon
her. We are going to stand by her, and do all
we can for her," Clement Doyle urged; "but we
cannot spoil our life because she is unhappy."

"We need not spoil our life, Clement. I am
not seven-and-twenty yet. I shall not be quite
an old woman at thirty. And it will be better
for you, perhaps, to be free and alone in India
while your great work is in progress."

Clement swallowed the passionate words that
rose up at this assertion. It vexed him to know
that there were a good many people he knew
who would agree with Dora, and think it to his
advantage to be without any domestic encum-
brances while his great work was going on. He
would be moving about—roughing it, living in
tents. Would it avail him much in the way of
happiness to have a wife up at the hills all
through the hot weather? Would not Dora,
safe in England, be a happier image in his
mind than Dora at Simla, or at Naini Tal, with

all the possibilities of fever, and with the spectre of cholera shadowing the scene? No! Those bugbears should not come between him and happiness! He wanted to take his wife to India with him. The idea of going back alone, the renunciation of that enchanting future they two had planned in the sunny days at Heatherside—the honeymoon tour in August and September, through the fair Oberland, and then to Lucerne, and across the Gotthard down to the romantic shores of Maggiore and Como—to renounce all this in order that his betrothed should do the work that was her sister's duty, and which ought to be her sister's one purpose in life! He had seen too little of Ellinor Lerwick to know, as Dora knew, how unschooled she was in a mother's duties—but he had seen enough at Heatherside, and heard enough in the careless talk of the boys, to know that Mrs. Lerwick was not a model mother. She appeared always at her best at Heatherside, from the motherly point of view. Her Palatine Square habits would have been a revelation to Clement Doyle.

"Clement, you know how dearly I love you, how grateful I am for your love."

"Grateful? No! no!"

"Yes, grateful—that you who are so good and so clever should care for little insignificant me. It was like a fairy tale. Cinderella, sitting by the kitchen fire, and sent away in a coach and six to shine at the Court Ball, could not have been more surprised than I was when you began to care for me."

"When I began! Why, there was no beginning. It was always. Yes, Dora, it *was* like a fairy tale. Do you remember the day I came to Mill Park? It was afternoon—and you were standing at a table at the end of the long drawing-room, pouring out tea for everybody—so graceful—so gracious—smiling at Sir Henry and the curate as they came to fetch the cups, talking in a low voice which I could only hear as a vague sweet sound in the distance. 'What little fairy is this?' thought I. Yes, that is the very name I gave you, Dora, the first time these eyes ever looked upon your fair young face, your sylph-like figure; and I made up my mind, very soon after, that if you were to be won you should be my good fairy.   And now you talk of deserting me—now, when our pathway through the world lies broad and smooth before us!"

" I waited for you, Clement," she said, gravely. " I only ask you to wait a few years for me."

"A few years.   Why, our lives will be spent in waiting.   This little woman talks of three years as lightly as if she were proposing a delay of six weeks."

"Clement, I am quite in earnest.   I cannot leave those boys till they are older; till they have settled prospects in life; till my sister has quite recovered from the shock of poor Tony's sad fate, and has grown accustomed to poverty, or to making the most of a very small income.   All that cannot be done in a few months."

" But it can in the best part of a year.   Suppose we sacrifice our honeymoon—Switzerland and the Italian lakes, the delicious tour we reckoned upon—and postpone our marriage till the beginning of October; and just go straight

away from Tilbury in the P. and O. Surely that
would be enough?"

"No, no, Clement, not nearly enough," she
answered, resolutely. "I have made up my
mind. When a great calamity comes upon a
family—as it has come upon us—we must kiss
the rod. I mean to devote the next three years
of my life to my sister and her children. I
have no fortune to give them; but I can give
them my care, and time, and love. I have been
with them in their sunshine. I will stop with
them in their shadow."

She broke down again just a little, and shed
some tears at this; but recovering herself quickly,
she took Clement Doyle's hand in hers and
smiled at him as she led him from the room.

"Come to the schoolroom tea," she said. "The
boys are expecting you. Don't be angry with
me, Clement. I have thought this business out
in many an anxious hour; and I know I could
do nothing less than I am going to do."

She did not tell him of those quiet hours of
prayer, in which she had supplicated for guidance,

and for the welfare and safety of the lover who was to go back to the land of many perils without her. She did not tell him of the tears she had shed over the happy dreams that were not to be fulfilled till years had come and gone. And who could tell what those unknown years might bring? What of disaster or disappointment?

Clement Doyle's appearance in the schoolroom was greeted with loud acclaim by the three boys. Each had something to say to him; each about his own business.

"I'm not going back to Elstree," said Eustace, "and I'm not going to Harrow or Oxford. We're all going to school in Cornwall, where Charles Kingsley went."

"Him that wrote 'Water Babies,'" said Fluff, eagerly.

Fluff had come upstairs to tea as a condescension, from the hot-house atmosphere of his mother's room, where the perfume of stephanotis that had blossomed last season seemed still to linger in the air; or it might be only the association of ideas which filled Ellinor Lerwick's boudoir with phantom odours.

Paul told Mr. Doyle, confidentially, that he was going to work for a scholarship; and that he meant to go to Oxford and get a first in classics ; and then he would go to the Bar.

"I don't mean my education to cost mother much," he said.

"Let it be the Indian Bar, Paul, and I may be able to help you."

"Yes, you could give me all your disputes about contracts and things, and your railway bills. I should like to begin one of the languages at once, if you'll lend me a Hindustani grammar."

" I'll do better than that, Paul. I'll be your Munshi."

Everybody brightened at his coming—even Miss Perry, who was modestly toasting buns while Sarah laid the tea-things. The boys wondered that they could still have buns, now that they were so poor; and then Paul remembered that Auntie had brought those buns in a bag from Bond Street, and had most likely paid for them out of her pocket-money. The schoolroom, with its low ceiling and common furniture, looked much pleasanter to-night than the drawing-rooms below-stairs in their melancholy abandonment.

There in the days gone by had been the stalled oxen; here was the lowly dinner of herbs, and contentment withal.

"We are all going to gran'pa's, Uncle Clem," said Fluff, when they were seated round the tea-table, Miss Perry at the teapot, and Auntie cutting bread and butter, whilst the toasted buns frizzled in front of the fire. "Are you coming, too?"

"I'm coming as far as Bideford, and you'll see me pretty often at Mill Park," answered Doyle.

"Our shelties are going to be sold," said Fluff, as if it were something to be cheerful about. "I'm rather glad, don't you know, for mine would soon have been getting too small for me."

"Somebody must find a couple of Exmoors for you and Paul," said Doyle.

"Oh, I shouldn't care about that, unless I could go out with the Devon and Somerset—

and Mill Park is too far from their meets. I don't care much for riding unless it's to hounds."

"Mother won't be able to keep ponies for us ever again," said Paul, "so there'd be no use in beginning. I'm sorry I didn't ride Roderick oftener while I had him."

Clement Doyle's presence among them cheered them all somehow. It was a relief to see some one who came from the outside world, who was not an inhabitant of that melancholy house. It was a relief to Fluff to have left his mother's room, and her tears and kisses, and to be able to prattle about himself, and what was going to happen to him—about what he was going to do in Cornwall if they went to Helstone, or at Bedford, or at Berkhampstead, or at any other school which might be ultimately chosen.

"Auntie isn't going to India never," concluded Fluff, triumphantly. "She's going to stay with us always."

"Never and always are words for the great Mogul. Sensible little boys know better than to use them," said Clement Doyle.

CHAPTER XVII.

NOT WITHOUT FRIENDS.

THERE was a great bustle next morning before the family got fairly under weigh for Bideford, in the South-Western express; but Aunt Dora's responsibilities were greatly lessened by Clement Doyle, who took entire charge of Mrs. Lerwick, the two dogs, and the luggage, leaving Dora free to devote herself to her nephews. Poor Mrs. Lerwick left Palatine Square crying silently behind her crape veil; but whether she was weeping for her husband's tragical fate, or for the loss of that luxurious home, and all the splendour and gaiety that had been her portion under that roof, nobody ever knew. She was silent and depressed, submitting to every arrangement that was made for her sons, but taking no

part in the business of their lives. Only now
and then did she smile, in the course of the
long journey, and then it was a wan little smile,
addressed exclusively to Fluff or her dog.
Perhaps during those few hours Clement Doyle
came to understand her helplessness and useless-
ness better than he could have understood from
anything that his betrothed told him about her.
He saw that she had to learn all a mother's
duties, to begin the alphabet of domestic life.

A surprise awaited Paul at Waterloo Station,
where a lady in grey met him on the platform,
and drew him aside into the obscurity of a
luggage-weighing office, and hugged him as she
had never hugged him in her life before.

"Oh, Miss Warren, I thought you'd forgotten
me!"

"Why, I called in Palatine Square every other
day, Paul, to ask after you and your poor mother.
Didn't Sarah tell you?"

"Not she. If you ever want to keep a secret,
give it to Sarah, in the shape of a message.
You may be quite sure it will be as safe as if

it were under the Great Pyramid. I'm glad you didn't quite forget us in our troubles."

"My dear, dear boy! Trouble has come upon you in the morning of your life, Paul; but trouble is a kind of education for the young. It braces and strengthens them for the battle of life. You are a clever boy, Paul, and I have taken pains with you. I think you know that."

"Yes, Miss Warren. I used to rather hate you for making a sap of me, but I'm glad of it now. There'll be no Christ Church for me, no Oxford or Cambridge, even; unless I can get scholarships, so as to cost mother hardly anything. But I mean to work hard wherever I am."

"That's my own brave boy! You can get a scholarship, and a fellowship by-and-by, if you work. It's in your power to do well, my dear. You'll write to your old governess sometimes, won't you, Paul? I shall be so glad to know how you get on. By-and-by, when you're a young man in London, a law student, perhaps, there'll always be room for you in my house."

"You're very kind. I always knew you were

good, don't you know; and I'll be sure to write and tell you of my prizes, and when I'm promoted to an upper form."

She gave him a bookseller's parcel.

"There are three of Carlyle's books that we have talked about, Paul. I should like you to read them sometimes, and to keep them always, as a souvenir of your old governess."

"I will, Miss Warren; and when I get my fellowship, you must come to Oxford and stay with me. You'll have to sleep outside, you know; but I can have you in my rooms all day, and grub you from the College kitchen."

"I shall be proud of your success, Paul. Hark, there's the bell, and here comes your Aunt looking for you. The basket is for the journey."

She put a neatly packed basket into his hand, kissed him, and hurried away, as Dora and Clement Doyle approached to fetch Paul. The travellers were all settled in their compartment, except Dora and Doyle.

"What a dear old thing Warren is," said Paul, as he and his brothers examined the contents of the basket, while the train glided out of the terminus with slow and stately motion. "A Dundee cake, scones cut open and buttered, apples, pears, sandwiches. And all so beautifully packed!"

"She's a human being after all," said Stacie. "I never should have thought it."

"Ah, you didn't understand her," retorted Paul. "And you didn't understand what she taught you."

"I didn't try to," replied his brother, bluntly, "I hated lessons with her just a little worse than in class at Elstree."

"You'll turn over a new leaf at Helstone, Stacie, for mother's sake," said Dora, in a low voice.

"Oh yes, we're poor now, and I shall have to swot. I never could see the fun of rich boys being saps."

"What a nice carriage—and engaged," said Fluff, beginning to pick off the label on the window. "And first-class! Paul said we was never to travel first-class no more."

"There's been a mistake, I'm afraid," said

T

Dora. "I gave Clement the money for second-class tickets. I must owe him a lot."

"Not a stiver," said Mr. Doyle, blushing and laughing a little. "The directors are friends of mine. This is a family carriage. First-class tickets for second-class fare."

"I shall always travel in a family carriage," said Fluff, complacently. "I hate cads."

"Oh, but you're a cad yourself now," said Stacie, "and you'll have to put up with them."

This was one of Stacie's coarse speeches, which his mother had been wont to protest against; but she uttered no reproof this morning. She was sitting in her comfortable corner, with her back to the engine, her head pillowed in a down cushion that had been as a grain of sand among the manifold luxuries of her morning room. She was trying to read the railway novel that Mr. Doyle had bought for her; but between the lines which she saw dimly, with eyes tired out by tears, there came the vision of the life that was to have been in this chill December; the white villa at Monte Carlo, the orange trees in blossom, the sapphire sea; and, more precious than sky and land and sea, the visitors, the luncheons, and evening parties, the dances, the gowns she was to have worn; and last, but, oh, not least, not quite the least of all, the fond, indulgent husband whose foolish life had ended in a flash of despair.

The boys enjoyed their journey, the country through which they were flying was so fair, even in its winter aspect. The sky was so different from the murky roof of London. They had come out of the house of gloom, and their hearts were gladdened. Stacie's feelings were warm; and Paul's feelings were very deep; even Fluff was sorry for the loss of the father who had never spoken an unkind word to his children, and who had thought of them about as seriously as if they had been a cage of canaries. Yes, all three boys were sorry; but youth is youth, and they enjoyed the journey, and the welcome in grandfather's comfortable house—quite a shabby house as compared with Heatherside, and governed by one elderly indoor servant, who called himself a butler, but whom Fluff discovered next morning in the boot-room cleaning the Squire's top-boots.

"Do you clean boots?" Fluff asked. "We had a young man on purpose. He did nothing all day but fill scuttles and clean boots; and Sarah said he was always complaining that he'd too much to do. You seem to do everything."

"I only look to the Squire's hunting things, Mr. Fritz. That have been my dooty ever since I come to Mill Park."

"Oh," said Fluff, "you must be a very useful man."

"I'm not ashamed of that, sir."

"Ain't you? Our servants couldn't bear to be useful—except Sarah. Sarah's a regular brick. She's going to stop with us now we're cads."

"Now you're what, Mr. Fritz?" asked Parker, horrified.

"Cads. Now we're poor. It's the same thing, don't you know."

"No it ain't, sir; there's rich cads and poor cads; but a gentleman is always a gentleman. Money don't make no difference."

"I'm glad of that, Parker. I thought Mother wouldn't be a lady any more—not a real lady—now she's had to leave Palatine Square, and now that all her furniture's going to be sold. I'm glad you think it won't make any difference."

"Not one little bit, Master Fritz. Your Ma is every inch a lady, and would be if she hadn't a sixpence. Why, I've waited upon her ever since she left the schoolroom, and there never was a more helpless young lady. I never knew her lift a finger for herself. Now Miss Hampden, she's very sweet and nice in her ways ; but she do lean to being a little bit common. There's nothing she won't put her hand to. I've seen her up with a dusting brush and go at the droring-room cabinets, if she see any dust on the old Dresden china—and having known her from a baby, I've made bold to say, 'That ain't your work, Miss Dorothea, and I'll let the housemaid have it warm for exposing you to the temptation.' But your Ma, Master Fritz, well she's a lady to the tips of her fingers. I don't believe she could pick up a pin with them."

CHAPTER XVIII.

SWEET USES OF ADVERSITY.

THE real beginning of the Lerwicks' new life
came about a month after Christmas, when they
migrated a good deal further west, still under
convoy of Aunt Dora and Clement Doyle, who
insisted upon sharing in all her more arduous
duties, declaring to everybody that he enjoyed the
fun of it, and that it was the best thing that could
happen to his liver; while to Dora's private ear
he urged that, like Ruth and Naomi, he would go
wherever she went, and her people should be his
people.

"And it will be hard if you and I can't settle
your sister and her sons comfortably before next
September," said Doyle, "so that you will be able
to leave them with an easy conscience."

No such argument, however tenderly urged, would avail with Dora. She had made up her mind to a certain act of self-sacrifice ; and nothing would turn her from the path of duty.

"You don't want me to go to India to be unhappy there, Clement," she said ; "and I should be unhappy if I were to leave the boys before they are a few years older, and before their mother has had time to grow into her new life."

How kindly the boys took to that new life ! How happy the people whose reverses of fortune come to them in their youth, while the human machine has the power of readjustment, the compensating movement which can fit itself to any phase of circumstances. Mrs. Lerwick felt the martyrdom of poverty in every hour of her existence. Her days were full of sharp pinpricks. The small rooms, the coarse linen, the common things that met her eye and touch at every turn, the smuts and smears on Sarah's morning face, everything irritated her. True that the carefully-chosen furniture was as pretty and artistic as inexpensive things could be, and that

Sarah's face and Sarah's cap were spotless at the early dinner, which Mother and Aunt now shared with the boys, and on the remains of which Sarah dined in her little kitchen, looking into the new-made garden, where neat borders had been filled with the hardy perennials that are the joy of homely gardeners. To Mrs. Lerwick's mind, that half-acre of garden with its coarse grass and herbaceous borders was horrible; for she could not look at it without thinking of the grounds and glass houses at Heatherside, where four under-gardeners had to stroll about with watering-pots and wheelbarrows all day, while three superior Scotchmen toiled or meditated in the seclusion of hot-houses and potting-sheds.

But while their mother moaned and remembered, the boys took to this new garden as kindly as if they had never seen a flower before. They declared that the grass was just big enough for what Stacie called nursery cricket, till Clement Doyle suggested bowls, when the mere utterance of this magic word was enough to turn all their attention to the mighty work of levelling the bowling green under Uncle Clem's supervision, Uncle Clem helping in the process himself with an energy that would have been creditable in an experienced navvy.

When the ground was made, he was to supply the bowls. They would come in time for Stacie's fourteenth birthday, at the end of March. They had little fear of frost in this far western region.

While the masculine mind was concentrated upon scalping and levelling, and brick-rubbish laying, and turfing, the little Auntie was just as hard at work on the flower borders, planting bush roses and southernwood, and sowing nasturtium seed and mignonette. That cheap glory of orange and yellow nasturtium was to spread itself all over the low granite wall, a brilliant background for the roses ; and at the end of the garden there was to be a row of sunflowers, of varieties which Dora begged of the cottagers whose acquaintance she had begun to make in every direction. And the corners were to be filled with marigolds. It was to be a yellow garden, Dora told her lover.

" My garden in the East will consist of a single

tree," said Clement. "I shall plant a willow and
sit under it, and think of the cruellest girl in the
world."

"Ah, but you know she isn't cruel," said Stacie ;
"she knew us ages before she knew you ; and she
isn't going to leave us till we're old enough to
take care of Mother."

They began their school career after Easter, by
which time all three, even to the petted Fluff, had
accepted small means as if they had been to the
manner born. They wore boots that had been
soled and heeled—a process they had never heard
of till they came to Helstone ; they were careful
of their clothes ; they ate the plainest dinners
with gusto, and never hinted at a wish for anything better than the boiled rice or cannon-ball
pudding, the dog-in-the-blanket, or currant dump-
lings, that varied the second course. Through
all the deprivation or carefulness of their young
lives ran the thought of helping Mother. They
were brave to bear anything, to do without anything, to work their hardest at the dullest lessons,

for Mother's sake. Dora had so impressed upon them the idea of the great sorrow that had fallen on their mother, which nothing but their love could lessen.

"She looks to you for consolation now, and happiness in the future," she told them; "and by-and-by, when I am in India——"

"Oh, that will be too horrid for words," interjected Stacie.

"She will have only you."

"Auntie," said Paul, thoughtfully, "isn't it rather mean of us to make Uncle Clem go back without you? We ought to be able to take care of Mother—we three."

"No, we can't," interposed Fluff; "besides, she" —indicating Dora—"makes all the cakes and pasties. She mustn't go."

Dora had developed a talent for cakes and pastry since they came to Helstone; and it was her light hand that made the blanket for the jam dog, and the crust for the savoury potato pasty, which was such a cheap addition to the homely tea. There were no late dinners at Fir Tree Cottage—only a

composite evening meal which Clement Doyle
called a thick tea, and pretended to enjoy
tremendously.

Fluff was reproved by both brothers as a selfish
little beggar.

"We ain't greedy like him, and we don't want
you to slave at pastry-making, little Auntie,"
explained Eustace; "but we do want you very
badly. It would be awful when Mother's low if
you weren't here."

Their mother's misery was a far worse ordeal
for the two elder boys than any trials of their own.
Ellinor Lerwick was subject to fits of "lowness";
a state of tearful apathy from which it was very
difficult to arouse her. It was very difficult on
these low days to persuade her to leave her own
room; to get up and dress herself and go into
the open air; almost impossible to induce her to
go out for a walk, though the air and the sky
and the racing clouds and racing waves and fresh
odours of newly-ploughed fields offered the very
finest restoratives for mind and body. It was
hard work to coax her to sit with them at their

meals when she was in this mood, though her absence made a painful gap in the small circle. The clatter of knives and forks was agony to her. If she were upstairs in her own room she would ring her bell with nervous vehemence, and send Sarah to entreat them all to make less noise. Their talk and laughter were torturing her.

Dora knew that if she were to leave her sister before she had risen superior to this sorrowful self-indulgence, the boys would be left almost entirely to Sarah's ministrations. Their mother would just shut herself in her room, and live in a low-spirited solitude; broken only by tearful interviews with Fluff. No, there was no help for it. Till her sister had learnt a mother's duties, Dora must stay. Were it seven years instead of three, she would serve her apprenticeship to adversity, and bear her portion of the sorrow that had fallen upon the helpless and weak.

There was not much weakness about the three boys when they made their first appearance in Helstone School, after the Easter holidays. The Cornish moors, the Cornish sands, the winds that blow over three thousand miles of ocean, had strengthened the youngest and frailest of them, and had developed Stacie into a young athlete. The boys had taken kindly to that wild western coast, the serpentine caves, the Lizard, with its tall twin lighthouses, and great ships for ever passing within signalling distance ; ships that told of welcome or farewell. The boys had begun almost to think themselves Cornishmen, and to talk of " All for One and One for All "; and they were proud to tell people that their grandfather's family had been settled in North Devon ever since the Great Rebellion.

They liked the school. Eustace had his own ideas of the difference between Elstree and Helstone ; but he kept them to himself, "for mother's sake." The other boys could make no comparisons. Paul was delighted to take up his classics again. He had been cramming himself with English History, and working at French with Aunt Dora during the interval. Fluff was charmed to find himself in a herd of other boys, and excited by the novel delights of a playground. Not one regret had Fluff for the velvet nest of his child-hood—the beautiful room, the shaded lamps, the perfume of gardenias, and the frequent entreaty to make less noise. Fluff playing games and screaming at the top of his shrill young voice, was a very different person to the languid child who had sprawled on the Persian carpet listlessly teasing Spitz, or looking about the room and taxing his young invention to discover some piece of mischief for idle hands to do.

A place had been found for Miss Perry in a vicar's family near Clovelly, and it had been settled that she was to spend all her holidays with the Lerwicks. She had no "people" of her own, or at any rate no people who wanted her for more than a week's visit, and she was very glad to know that Mrs. Lerwick's house would be her holiday home till the boys were grown up.

"I'm sure I'll work my fingers to the bone to be useful to you, Mrs. Lerwick," she said, "for I do love you with all my heart;" and that was about the most energetic speech that little Miss Perry had ever made since the Lerwicks had known her.

When the summer vacation began Miss Perry appeared with a trunk and bonnet-box, and the little Auntie disappeared the day after. The boys thought the governess a very poor exchange for their Aunt; but the pain of parting had been lessened by much talk of reunion at the end of the holidays, and Dora's nephews agreed that it was only right she should go home to be with the Squire for a little time. He must have missed her awfully at breakfast and dinner—the only periods at which he wanted feminine society; for he was out-of-doors all day, and spent his evenings in the billiard-room reading the papers, or dozing over a volume of the *Old Sporting Magazine*, to which his father had been an occasional contributor.

There were to be guests at Mill Park. Lady Mandeville had brought home a little boy and an Ayah, and Sir Henry was to come home in the spring, and he and his wife were to go back to India the following autumn, possibly leaving the little boy with his grandfather, and then, perhaps, Miss Perry might be engaged as his governess. Dora had this possibility in her mind.

Clement Doyle was invited to meet Lady Mandeville, and a couple of cousins, male and female, were to make up the party. And then in September, about the end of the holidays, Clement and his sweetheart were to bid each other good-bye; and Dora was to go back to Helstone for the winter, while Lady Mandeville stayed at Mill Park, to take care of her father at breakfast and dinner.

All this time Mrs. Lerwick's income had been made up for her by voluntary contributions from her father and her sisters, of which the widow herself knew very little, Dorothea managing all financial matters for her.

"There is no need for you to trouble, dearest, till everything is settled," Dora told her. "When the two houses have been sold, and the lawyers have paid all the creditors, and made up their accounts, you shall know exactly what remains for you and the boys. You are not going to be left in the dark, Nell. We all want you to be a woman of business, and to keep accounts, and to manage your income."

"I must learn subtraction," Ellinor answered, with a puzzled brow; "I don't make many mistakes in addition, but I can't subtract. To take one pound eleven and sixpence from two pounds ten! It's horrid having to borrow the eighteen-pence. Of course, I must keep accounts, if there are any to be kept; but I dare say when everybody has been paid the lawyers will take all that is left, and the boys and I will be paupers, dependent upon you and Father and the Mandevilles to keep us out of the workhouse."

"No, no, dearest, it won't be as bad as that; and even if you and the boys were penniless, we should all love to help you."

"Better than I should love to be helped," the widow answered bitterly.

She threw her arms round Dora's neck, apologetically, the next minute.

"I'm not ungrateful, dear. I'm only miserable," she said.

Happily, there was something left from the wreck of Anthony Lerwick's princely income. The sale of the house in Palatine Square and all its costly contents realized a large sum of money ; for the Lerwick china and pictures were sold at Christie's, and that passing herd, who had been entertained in Ellinor Lerwick's golden days, went about London talking of those Lerwicks, and the monstrous rate at which they had lived, and so advertised the sale, and brought a mob of smart people to outbid each other for modern Sèvres vases and Dresden teacups made the year before last, while some of the really choice things were bought at sensational prices. The Dorsetshire estate also sold better than had been expected, since the extension and development of Bournemouth had tripled the value of the Heatherside home farm, with its frontage to the roads between Branksome and Poole. And then there were stables and a bachelor's box at Newmarket, which Mr. Lerwick had furnished before his marriage. There was "the valuable racing stud of a gentleman deceased," and there were Ellinor Lerwick's jewels, the greater number of which were bought by her sisters. Altogether the breaking up of this fortune produced a large sum of money, and after every creditor had been paid in full there remained a balance of twelve thousand pounds for the widow, which, invested in railway stock of the first quality, would secure her about four hundred a year.

The income would be hers, unfettered by trustees, for Anthony Lerwick had made only one will since his marriage, and that left everything to his wife, without reservation. He had been too deeply in love to speculate on the chances of the future, too happy in the present to think of death, or of change.

" The capital as well as the income will be in your power, Ellinor," Mr. Hampden said, solemnly, when he came to Helstone to explain things to his daughter ; "any folly of yours might make your children beggars. If you were to marry again, for instance. . . ."

" Marry again ! As if there were another man in this world like Tony," sobbed the widow.

That idea of her children's fate being dependent upon her had a steadying effect upon Mrs. Lerwick's mind. Gradually, as the year wore on, her agony of regret for the splendours of the past abated, and all that brilliant life of the London season, the visiting and entertaining, the dressing and dancing, the perpetual movement and glitter, began to seem like a dream she had dreamt, or a fashionable novel that she had read. Gradually the dim, untried soul awakened to a sense of her children's claims upon her, and a just appreciation of their love and tender care for her—Eustace so bold and brave and eager to protect her; Paul so watchful and apprehensive of anything that could worry or pain her; Fritz so fond and clinging, so delicately sensitive of her sorrow. Yes, she told herself, in these sons of hers she had treasures more precious than her "position" in society, her three drawing-rooms, or the dazzling array of her silver tables. The things that she had lost were as dust and ashes compared with this living love which wrapped her round with its gentle warmth, this bright white light of brain and heart which shone upon her humble pathway. Sometimes, too, philosophy, a feminine philosophy, would come to the aid of affection and right feeling. "Even if

we had always been rich, I should have grown old,"
she reflected, " I should have grown too old for my
frocks ; and I should have had to go to balls and
dinners with scraggy shoulders, and a withered
throat that all my necklaces could not hide.   I am
almost glad I had to part with my jewels before I
was old.   I have so often laughed at old women
covered with diamonds, and looking like Egyptian
mummies."

Clement Doyle escorted his sweetheart back to
Helstone when the holidays were over ; and after
he had brought her there it took him nearly three
weeks to say good-bye.   He was resigned now to
the inevitable.   Dora's firmness had conquered
him ; but he told Stacie in confidence that he,
Stacie, would have to make haste and grow
up, as in all probability that engineering job in
Lahore would get itself finished in two years
instead of three, and then the little Auntie would
be wanted.

" Don't you be afraid," said Stacie.   " You've
acted like a brick in letting her stop with us ; and

Paul and I will do all we can to make Mother's life happy ; so that she'll be able to spare Auntie when you come back. It was a sell, though, her getting engaged ; because we all counted upon her being an old maid, and living with us to the end of the chapter."

" And having to put up with the airs and graces of her three nephews' wives ! That's apt to be a very dull kind of chapter, Stacie. When Dora goes out to India with me she'll be a little queen ; and grey-headed old Generals and long-headed old Civilians will bow down and worship her, and the young men at the station will think it a privilege to dance attendance upon her."

" When there are babies she'll have to bring 'em home. That's one jolly good job," said Stacie waxing malicious.

" You'll be coming out to us before then, perhaps, if you do well at Cooper's Hill," answered Mr. Doyle.

Dora's work prospered. The trees and flowers flourished in the Helstone garden. Myrtle and jasmine, clematis and wisteria spread their broad mantle of colour over the dull grey of the shabby stone house ; and pretty little bits of old-fashioned furniture and oriental china that could be spared from Mill Park made Mrs. Lerwick's drawing-room an apartment to be praised by the nicest people in the neighbourhood.

When the boys had been two years at Helstone school, and Mrs. Lerwick had exchanged her first deep mourning for a simple black gown and a neat little black straw bonnet, she had her circle of friends, who were as exalted in their rural distinction as the smart people who had visited her, and looked down upon her, in Palatine Square. She had a small circle of friends whose names began with Tre, Pol, and Pen, and who had insisted upon being kind to Mr. Hampden's widowed daughter, and in drawing her as much as possible out of her sad seclusion in the small grey house near the school. Her pale and pensive beauty, her gentle manners, pleased all the nicest people. She was voted "interesting," and was petted by everybody; wondered at and lauded for her perfect management of her house and her sons.

"I dare say that pretty little sister helps her a good deal," suggested Lady Penlyon to Mrs. Trequite.

"I don't know about helping her! She plays tennis and even cricket with the boys, and is more of a tom-boy than one quite likes a person of that age to be," replied Mrs. Trequite.

Whereby it may be seen that Dorothea's devotion to her sister, and her sister's interests, had been so unobtrusively rendered as to have won no renown for her in the neighbourhood. She was worshipped by all the young men, who told each other disgustedly that she was engaged to some beggar in India; but the matrons thought of her somewhat lightly, as a giddy-pated young woman who cared for nothing but golf and afternoon tea.

"She is in her glory pouring out tea, with half a dozen young men to fetch and carry for her," said Mrs. Trequite, the adoring mother of three plain daughters; and the feminine high court of justice agreed that it was a great advantage for such a frivolous little person to live with that sweet serious widowed sister.

Nobody ever suspected that for the greater part of her sojourn at Helstone, Dora had managed every detail of the family life.

The time came, happily for them all, when she was able to hand over the keys and the account-books, and to commit the welfare of her nephews to their mother's hands, knowing that adversity's rough lessons had been taken to heart, and that the feather-headed Mrs. Lerwick, of Palatine Square, had slowly and gradually developed into the tender and thoughtful mother of three affectionate sons. The change in Fluff was no less complete than the change in Fluff's mother. The conceit and arrogance, which were the growth of years of foolish indulgence, had been knocked out of him in a month's experience of a rough-and-ready public school. Boys whose social position he considered immeasurably below his own, thrust out a derisive tongue on the smallest manifestation of "swagger" or "side" on his part;

and this vulgar and primitive argument, which at first reduced him to tears, was later accepted as a challenge to single combat. The effeminacy of the spoiled child gave place to a too ardent combativeness, which had to be restrained by home influence. And if the rough-and-tumble of the playground cured him of pride and vanity, it was home influence—the knowledge of his mother's deprivations—that cured him of selfishness. In those little voluntary sacrifices—so futile and so sweet—which children make for those they love, he learnt the habit of self-denial; and the Fritz of the second year at Helstone Grammar School was a very different boy to the Fluff who had sprawled with listless limbs on the Indian prayer-rug in Mrs. Lerwick's morning room. Poverty teaches in a hard school; but when poverty does not mean actual stint, or the terror of debt, it is about the best master childhood and youth can have; and Ellinor Lerwick's fatherless boys showed themselves apt pupils, and took very kindly to the lesson.

"It's ever so much jollier here than it was in

Palatine Square; and we get more fun here than at Heatherside."

That was the verdict of the three boys on the eve of Dora's departure for Mill Park, a few weeks before her wedding-day. Clement Doyle had managed to get the big work finished in less than three years, and he had come back to claim his bride. The work had been done well, and the engineer had considerably improved his position and money-earning power, so that, as Lady Mandeville wrote patronizingly in a letter to her father, it really was "a very good match for dear little Dora, and a connection that our family has no reason to be ashamed of; and I have no doubt that Clement Doyle will be able to be very useful to those poor boys whom Dora makes such a foolish fuss about. Of course, they will have to rough it, whatever they go in for, and if they come out here they mustn't expect life to be a bed of roses, any more than it is in England."

LONDON: PRINTED BY WILLIAM CLOWES AND SONS, LIMITED, STAMFORD STREET AND CHARING CROSS.

Miss Braddon's Novels.

List, &c., &c.

MISS BRADDON'S NOVELS.

THE AUTHOR'S AUTOGRAPH EDITION.

2s. 6d. each, cloth gilt.   2s. each, picture boards.

1. LADY AUDLEY'S SECRET.
2. HENRY DUNBAR.
3. ELEANOR'S VICTORY.
4. AURORA FLOYD. [LEGACY.
5. JOHN MARCHMONT'S
6. THE DOCTOR'S WIFE.
7. ONLY A CLOD.
8. SIR JASPER'S TENANT.
9. TRAIL OF THE SERPENT.
10. LADY'S MILE.
11. LADY LISLE.
12. CAPTAIN OF THE VULTURE.
13. BIRDS OF PREY.
14. CHARLOTTE'S INHERITANCE.
15. RUPERT GODWIN.
16. RUN TO EARTH.
17. DEAD SEA FRUIT.
18. RALPH THE BAILIFF.
19. FENTON'S QUEST.
20. LOVELS OF ARDEN.
21. ROBERT AINSLEIGH.
22. TO THE BITTER END.
23. MILLY DARRELL.
24. STRANGERS AND PILGRIMS.
25. LUCIUS DAVOREN.
26. TAKEN AT THE FLOOD.
27. LOST FOR LOVE.
28. A STRANGE WORLD.
29. HOSTAGES TO FORTUNE.
30. DEAD MEN'S SHOES.
31. JOSHUA HAGGARD.
32. WEAVERS AND WEFT.
33. AN OPEN VERDICT.
34. VIXEN.
35. THE CLOVEN FOOT.
36. THE STORY OF BARBARA.
37. JUST AS I AM.
38. ASPHODEL.
39. MOUNT ROYAL.
40. THE GOLDEN CALF.
41. PHANTOM FORTUNE.
42. FLOWER AND WEED.
43. ISHMAEL.
44. WYLLARD'S WEIRD.
45. UNDER THE RED FLAG.
46. ONE THING NEEDFUL.
47. MOHAWKS.
48. LIKE AND UNLIKE.
49. THE FATAL THREE.
50. THE DAY WILL COME.
51. ONE LIFE, ONE LOVE.
52. GERARD.
53. THE VENETIANS.
54. ALL ALONG THE RIVER.
55. THOU ART THE MAN.
56. SONS OF FIRE.

Now ready.

SONS OF FIRE.

Cloth gilt, 2s. each.   Picture boards, 2s.

LONDON: SIMPKIN, MARSHALL, HAMILTON, KENT & CO., LTD.

LONDON PRIDE.

Large Crown 8vo. Cloth gilt, gilt top, 6s.

"It is really an astonishing performance."—*World.*

"Altogether the book is a remarkable one, even among the finest triumphs of this popular novelist's art."—*St. James's Gazette.*

"The delineation of Hyacinth is the real triumph of a book rich in minor successes."—*Pall Mall Gazette.*

"At the writer's vital touch the past springs into life, fresh and vivid as if it were but that of yesterday. It is a captivating book, vibrating with colour and life."—*Daily News.*

"'London Pride' is delightful to read, and especially delightful to those who like to be snatched away, as by some magical process, out of the present into times 'When the World was Younger.'"—*Daily Chronicle.*

"It will be plain from the extracts that the story is strong in thrilling situations. In addition to the exciting scenes already alluded to, there might be mentioned the rescue of Angela and her niece from the secret chamber known as the 'Priest's Hole;' and the dramatic account of Fareham's trial, where Angela perjures herself to screen the man she loves. Some of the descriptive passages, also, are worthy of special attention, notably that of the plague-stricken city."—*Literary World.*

"What would have been the reception of this novel had it been published anonymously? It is so different in subject from most of Miss Braddon's other novels that the experiment might well have been tried. We fancy that as an anonymous work 'London Pride' could not but have touched the public with the thought, 'Here, indeed, is a new writer who is head and shoulders above her contemporaries.'"—*Glasgow Herald.*

"However, there will be no difference of opinion among those best competent to judge. Miss Braddon is a past-master—there is but one sex in art—of the craft of story-telling, and that is evidenced in her latest effort, 'London Pride; or, When the World was Younger.'"—*Daily Telegraph.*

"Miss Braddon is undoubtedly a remarkably versatile writer. She has established herself easily first in the English novel of intrigue, for no one else can weave an intricate plot with so delicate and so adroit a hand."—*Manchester Guardian.*

"The tale of the love of Angela and Lord Fareham is dealt with strongly and faithfully; but this story of the unhappy love of a great-hearted, strong-headed man for a good woman, though a fine exercise in psychologic analysis, pales in interest before the cleverness that can rouse our sympathy for the foolish, feather-headed wife, struggling in the throes of her life's one passion."--*Pall Mall Gazette.*

"The glimpses which we get of my Lady Castlemaine and other fine ladies of the Court and the *haut monde* are fascinating to a degree, and had he but possessed the literary gift of construction as does our novelist of to-day, we could imagine garrulous, shrewd little Samuel Pepys writing such a story as 'London Pride.'"—*Court Journal.*

"We are sure that it will find as many admirers as its author's well-won reputation deserves."—*Westminster Gazette.*

"The story in itself is one of strong passion and sentiment, which would fit any period, and rich enough in incident to be independent of its gorgeous surroundings."—*Morning Post.*

"Full of interest alike as a novel and a reflex of English life—'When the World was Younger.'"—*Liverpool Courier.*

"The story, it goes without saying, is dramatic and of unflagging interest, but it is not only in the unravelling of the plot that readers will take delight, but in the side-lights on well-known places and persons."—*Gentlewoman.*

"Miss Braddon still preserves her admirable versatility and freshness, and in every page of her latest book will be detected that mastery of characterisation and descriptive power which have ever been the attributes of this clever novelist."—*Era.*

"It is a sorrowful, soothing, and delightful story."—*St. James's Budget.*

"It has other and higher qualities which demand a meed of admiration."—*Spectator.*

"A very vivid and sprightly picture of life in London under Charles II."—*Standard.*

"At the head of the list stands Miss Braddon's 'London Pride.'"—*Review of Reviews.*

"The tale is full of movement and vigour."—*Globe.*

"The version of the Stuart Period is a rare one, and it will vastly charm."—*Irish Times.*

"The story is told in Miss Braddon's best style."—*Weekly Sun.*

"'London Pride' is full of beauty."—*Black and White.*

LONDON: SIMPKIN, MARSHALL, HAMILTON, KENT & CO., LTD.

Sons of Fire.

" If the true office and function of a story is to serve as an anodyne, to take us out of the ordinary paths of humdrum existence and make us familiar with elemental passions; if, above all, its chief feature is not to discuss either a question of meta-physics or a problem of sex, but to intoxicate us with the heady fumes of romance—then we may be indeed thankful to Miss Braddon for having proved once more that she is a teller of stories in the old and familiar sense, a weaver of interesting plots, full of characteristic deftness and ingenuity."—*Daily Telegraph*.

" It is told with a charm and power which make its interest increase at a rapid rate as the story goes on. . . . The author of this story has given many good novels to the world, but none more likely to please and charm readers of all tastes."—*Scotsman*.

" In point of strong characterization, continuous interest, and clever development of plot, the story is equal to the very best from her gifted pen."—*People*.

" 'Sons of Fire' will surely commend itself to the very large circle of Miss Braddon's admirers."—*Lloyd's Weekly Newspaper*.

" In 'Sons of Fire,' her new novel, Miss Braddon departs from her usual method of treatment, and selects new ground for action. We are not taken at once into the centre of the web; and the scene of the most stirring events is a vast region of Central Africa, where Englishmen are known as the 'Sons of Fire.' This novel may rank with many of its predecessors in sustained interest. The rival suitors of Suzette—who will be a first favourite among the well-stocked ' garden of girls ' which Miss Braddon has provided for our pleasure—and their several mothers, Lady Emily Carew and Mrs. Wornock, are admirably drawn, while the plot, which comprises a strange physiological problem, is developed with the author's unfailing power and ability."—*The World*.

" The story is full of exciting situations, which Miss Braddon describes with familiar power, and a vigour and resource which command the reader's attention throughout."—*Leeds Mercury*.

" All who are in quest of a story well told and well worth the telling and the reading, will there find what they seek."—*Freeman's Journal*.

" Miss Braddon has lost none of the skill which won for her long ago a pre-eminent place among contemporary story-tellers. ' Sons of Fire ' is an admirable specimen of her art."—*Sunday Sun*.

" Plot is always Miss Braddon's strong point, and her skill has not failed her in ' Sons of Fire.' "—*Standard*.

" Thirty-five years of literary production have not dulled Miss Braddon's inventive power, or deadened her style. Her plot, her characters, the dramatic turn of incidents, the power of vivid and startling presentation, are as ' taking' as ever in this, her latest story. The book is artistically constructed. Our interest in the personages is awakened at the outset, the reader's curiosity piqued, at first by situations proper to light comedy, but gradually deepening and darkening in character till we reach the climax in the final chapters of the book."—*Birmingham Daily Post*.

" Miss Braddon's hand has not lost its cunning. Her devoted readers will find the story irresistible."—*Yorkshire Post*.

"How great, then, should be the power of a novelist, a teller of stories, who possesses style, originality, and grammar in addition to a gift of story-telling which has stood the test of a quarter of a century or more, and remains as indisputable as ever. Miss Braddon's latest romance, 'Sons of Fire,' shows no falling off in her fine gift of story-telling."—*Court Journal.*

"If my readers want a 'good novel'—and who does not?—they could not do better than order 'Sons of Fire.'"—*Glasgow Daily Record.*

"The authoress of 'Lady Audley's Secret' and a host of other novels too numerous to name, is to be congratulated on her latest venture. In fact, Miss Braddon has never written a better book than the 'Sons of Fire.'"—*Illustrated Sporting and Dramatic News.*

"If, however, you prefer to unbend your mind with a novel, you cannot do better than order the ever-young, inventive, and vigorous Miss Braddon's latest novel, 'Sons of Fire.'"—*Truth.*

Thou Art the Man.

"Without any exception that we can call to mind, Miss Braddon's fictional works —the name of which is legion—have always recommended themselves to the novel-reading public by the intrinsic strength and careful construction of their plots, and by the profusion of stirring incident with which the interest of their respective narratives is sustained and varied. These salient characteristics of her earlier productions are conspicuously displayed in Miss Braddon's latest story. . . . This strange story is told throughout with bright and unflagging spirit."—*Daily Telegraph.*

"Among the series of novels due to Miss Braddon's pen, none has been more full of human interest than 'Thou Art the Man.'"—*Morning Post.*

All Along the River.

"'All Along the River' is one of the most pathetic stories Miss Braddon has written. . . . The situation is natural, or, at any rate, quite conceivable, and there are not many, even of our latter-day weavers of romance, who could have traced it from beginning to end with so much grace and power as the author has brought to the elaboration of her idea."—*Athenæum.*

"In dramatic force and construction 'All Along the River' will compare not unfavourably with Miss Braddon's most popular works ; while in finish and refinement the book reaches a very high level."—*St. James's Gazette.*

"The indefatigable author of 'Lady Audley's Secret' and so many other old friends dear to us all loses none of her vigour and ingenuity as her books increase and multiply."—*Queen.*

"'All Along the River' shows no falling off on the part of its writer. From a literary point of view it is better than her earlier work, and for grace and tenderness leaves little to be desired. . . . The story is written with unmistakable power."—*Standard.*

"Few writers could have told the story of Isola's life so delicately and pathetically as Miss Braddon."—*Court Circular.*

The Venetians.

"The story, it need not be said, is exciting and full of plot, and it is worked out with all the ingenuity that the author has taught her readers to expect from her. There are nearly all the good features of a Braddonian story in 'The Venetians,' amongst them being a remarkable and never-failing freshness in the dialogues and descriptions, which make a novel by the author of 'Lady Audley's Secret' invariably pleasant reading."—*Athenæum.*

"'The Venetians' is almost as good as Miss Braddon's best. It shows her to have lost none of her talent for ingenious construction, none of her capacity for luxuriant description, none of her power of assimilating the fashions, the spirit, and the jargon of the hour."—*Times.*

"The story flows on uninterruptedly, with a skilful manipulation of the stream of incident which has come not only from instinct, but from practice. Miss Braddon is a much better artist now than she was when she wrote 'Lady Audley's Secret.'"—*Globe.*

"The plot is exciting, the word-painting and dialogues are fresh and vivid. The drama is evolved with the skill of an author unrivalled in the art of story-telling."—*Daily News.*

"There is no disguising the practised hand of Miss Braddon. It would be hard to compute the many weary brains which have been soothed by her facile and able pen. It is marvellous to note the immense strides this writer has made from the time when her early and powerful fictions showed a certain lack of maturity from the literary point of view, to the present time, when she adds her thorough experience in the 'craft' to those undoubted gifts which would have come to the front in any case, but possibly with less of absolute finish and success than the fiction-reading world is proud to accord to all she touches. That the author should be at home in Venice is not surprising—where would not that bright spirit be at home? And the reader is made at home too in a manner that fascinates. . . . So I leave this most powerful, most pathetic, and beautiful work, in which the reader will find a thousand charms, and on which I have no space to dwell, but of which I am fully sensible."—*Manchester Courier.*

LONDON: SIMPKIN, MARSHALL, HAMILTON, KENT & CO., LTD.